Praise for *The Ragged Way People Fall Out of Love*

"Succeeds hugely....When bad things happen to these people, your blood jumps. You are made to care about them that much, and I know of no higher praise you can give a book."

—Richard Bausch, *Washington Post Book World*

"Has the clean lines, the counterpoint of shadow and light and the sense of solitude edging into loss of an Edward Hopper painting."

—*New York Times Book Review*

"Only in art can the mistakes of our lives be measured with such grace and forgiveness, or redeemed through such close attention."

—*The New Yorker*

"In an age of mindless bulky page-turners, this was a rare and welcome experience.... If you think there's nothing fresh to say about married people who wake up one day and discover they don't want to be married anymore, think again. Better yet, read Elizabeth Cox."

—*Chicago Tribune*

"A novel of sparkling originality and depth."

—*San Francisco Chronicle Book Review*

"Beguiling."

—*San Diego Tribune*

"[Cox's] foray into the realm of the heart is symphonic, building slowly from an elegant, cool introduction to a fiery climax."

—*Booklist*

THE RAGGED
WAY PEOPLE FALL
OUT OF LOVE

A NOVEL BY

ELIZABETH COX

Harper Perennial
A Division of HarperCollins Publishers
An Edward Burlingame Book

HarperCollins books may be purchased for educational, business, or sales promotional use. For information, please call or write: Special Markets Department, HarperCollins Publishers, Inc., 10 East 53rd Street, New York, NY 10022. Telephone: (212) 207-7528; Fax: (212) 207-7222.

First HarperPerennial edition published 1992.

Designed by David Bullen

LIBRARY OF CONGRESS CATALOG CARD NUMBER 91-50513

ISBN 0-06-097454-0

92 93 94 95 96 97 CWI 10 9 8 7 6 5 4 3

For my brothers
Herbert Bernard Barks, Jr.
Coleman Bryan Barks

Why does the eye see things more clearly in
dreams than the imagination when awake?

THE NOTEBOOKS OF LEONARDO DA VINCI

THE RAGGED WAY PEOPLE FALL OUT OF LOVE

CHAPTER
ONE

"I don't love you anymore," William told Molly one Sunday afternoon as they sat together in the den. His eyes had a glass-slick look, strong with conscience. "It comes down to that, I think." He smiled. She wanted to ask him why he smiled. She knew he didn't mean to. They could hear the children playing volleyball on a neighbor's court, and Molly looked out the window, northward. She tried not to seem surprised. She didn't believe him anyway.

They had stopped arguing about anything, months ago, and instead became strictly critical of each other. "I'm not important to you, Will," Molly said repeatedly. She made it come true. "You don't trust me," William told her, and that came true too.

As he spoke about not loving her anymore, William's mouth looked peculiar and reasonable, but his tone of voice made Molly think that maybe he had said something else. The air held a bad secret for them, and she didn't want to hear the children playing. She got up to close the window on that day's bright sky, and turned.

"Why?" she asked him. His head and shoulders bent toward the floor and his hair stuck out on one side in a way that made Molly want to smooth it. But all she could think of was—Is this the first time in all these years he has ever felt that way? Because she had felt that way many times, though never felt the necessity to say it.

She blushed when he said he didn't love her, the same way she blushed eighteen years ago when he told her for the first time that he did love her, and it was what she wanted to hear. Now, the reasons he gave for not loving didn't make sense to her, though she could see by his expression that they made sense to him.

Molly couldn't say how she loved him. They seemed to be talking about something else, so even if she had said it, that wouldn't be what he wanted to hear. He wanted out. He had the look of someone in a cage who wanted out.

"All right," she said. But that was six months ago, and they didn't discuss at all when he would leave, so Molly hoped he might get over not loving her as someone might get over a short-term illness.

It was the year of Halley's comet, and the end of March. Molly could not describe how she felt anymore. The only time she understood completely was when she woke suddenly at four a.m., unprotected by the veils that kept her mind covered in the day. She felt the delicate fact of Will's body beside her in bed. He slept, sometimes touching her leg in an old way, and Molly's mind ran the spectrum of emotions from unreasonable to strangely sane.

"Is it time to get up?" William said. She hadn't known he was awake.

"Not yet." It was five-thirty. She lay awake until the sun rose. She would drive to Savannah today to see her father. Last night he'd called Molly and cried into the phone. Molly's mother died a year ago in April, and Frank Bates lived alone now. He wanted somebody to hear him when he said he planned to clean out the attic. "I think it's time to clear it out," he said. Then he added, "I don't want to do this part alone."

The sky in Stringer's Ridge, North Carolina, was brilliant with bright flecks and prophecy, and the weather this March was unseasonably warm. By seven-fifteen Molly had prepared three school lunches and one for the road. She had a sandwich, an apple, and cookies in a sack. She placed the sack beside her clothes.

"Can I go?" Lucas closed his mother's suitcase and sat on it, begging. "I didn't go last time." Lucas was seven, and Molly had already told him he couldn't go.

"Not this time, honey. I told you." He didn't like to stay home with his brother and sister and dad. They always forgot about him. Molly wished she could take him with her. She wanted to hear his mild chatter all the way to Georgia. Lucas could lift her heart and reduce all error.

"If I went, I could do things to help." He couldn't think of any specific thing.

"I know you could," Molly said. "You could do lots of things." Lucas rolled off onto the floor and stared at something. He was small and had a gift for being able to sit motionless with his eyes fixed on a spot on the rug or a tree outside the window, a bush— seeing, but seeing something in himself at the same time.

Molly sat at her dressing table. "You'll be late for school if you don't hurry," she said. Sunlight came in on her hair, like catching quick fire—her hair red and bushy with bright tangles. She tied it back with a yellow ribbon and put makeup on her cheeks. As a teenager, she had won a beauty contest, but she only thought of that sometimes when she saw new wrinkles around her mouth and eyes. She was forty-two. Her eyes were copper-colored, and she had low, straight-fringed brows that gave her face a serious look.

"Is Papa Frank sick?" Lucas asked.

"No."

"Franci said he might be sick."

Franci came into her mother's room. She was twelve and, because of that, liked to boss people around. "If Lucas's going, I get to go too." She had William's dark hair, which hung thinly around her shoulders. It didn't curl like her mother's, so each morning she woke early enough to curl it, then sprayed the curls to the stiffness of a wig. She wore a T-shirt that hung to her knees. It belonged to Joe, and Molly asked if Joe knew she was wearing it.

"He's not even awake yet," Franci said in her own defense.

William came out of the shower. He dressed without speaking, but Molly made a few halfhearted attempts at conversation. The children left the room.

Whenever Molly and William were alone together, they struggled with a politeness that had grown up between them. If William brushed against Molly in the hallway or the kitchen, they both quickly, the minute they touched, said, "Oh, sorry," as if they shouldn't have touched each other at all—that maybe there was even some rudeness to it, or as if one of them might have been bruised from that light contact.

"Is Joe up yet?" Molly called to Franci.

"He's up," Joe called back about himself. "Do I have to take everybody to school again?"

"Probably." If Franci and Lucas missed the bus, Joe drove them. His impatience about having to do this was uneven. He got up, but his alarm rang while he was in the bathroom and William turned it off.

Molly closed her suitcase and pulled it toward the stairs. She hoped William might ask her not to be gone long.

"I'll do that," William said.

"Oh, thank you."

William put on a blue shirt. It was new and Molly wondered when he'd bought it. It fit snug on his shoulders and he buttoned the cuffs instead of rolling them up as he usually did.

"You look nice," she told him. She had stepped out of the shower and was naked, dripping wet. Her hair was pushed high onto her head and held in place with bobby pins. Long tendrils fell out, wet on the ends. She never dried off. She liked to dress and let her clothes dry her body. William used to laugh at the foolish luxury of this habit, but now he wanted her to stop.

"Why don't you dry yourself off?" he asked. It was something he had loved years ago, and Molly didn't recognize now how he disliked it. During the past year they had been waking at night, both of them, as though an end were coming, as though they expected it to come in the night and surprise them. They didn't yet realize the ragged way people fall out of love and how it is never completely done.

Franci brought her mother a coin she would send to Papa Frank. He saved coins. This one was small and brass, the size of a postage stamp. Franci had something else too—a paper with two sentences written in a careful hand. For two years Franci had kept a record of particular sayings from a book she refused to name. She memorized these quotes with the seriousness of Bible verses, and asserted them in conversation as she thought of them.

At the supper table she might say, *"A panther will still fight with dogs and hunters after its entrails have fallen out,"* or *"A wild boar cures its diseases by eating ivy."*

"Where do you get that stuff?"

She wouldn't tell but admitted it all came out of the same book— "Not the encyclopedia," she said. She copied two more for Papa Frank. Sometimes he sent a quote back to her. Franci said he made it up, but he said it was from a real book like hers.

"Read them to me," Molly said. She loved Franci's quotes and said that in fact some of them sounded familiar to her. "I'm going to figure it out one of these days." In a way she hoped she wouldn't.

"One is long," Franci said, and didn't read it. It gave instructions on How to Make a Pontoon. The other she read: "Why is the fish in the water swifter than the bird in the air when it ought to be the contrary, seeing the water is heavier and thicker than the air, and the fish is heavier and has smaller wings than the bird?"

Lucas said he didn't have anything to send. He said what could he send, and grew whiny. He felt so easily defeated by Franci and tried hard to think of something. If he could think of something, he would give it. Lucas would give anything he had.

What he chose, the only thing he could finally come up with, was a shirt with "Redskins" on the back.

"Papa will love this," Molly said. She placed the shirt and coin carefully in her suitcase and put the quotes into her purse.

"Do you think Papa Frank will die?" Franci liked to talk about death. She had never seen anyone die, except on TV.

"No," Molly told her. "He's just lonely." She debated whether or not to take a dress. Joe came in ready for school. Molly felt scooped out every time she saw him. He was so handsome. He saw Franci wearing his T-shirt, and he pretended to care.

"Hey, Butt-face, is that mine?" He pulled her to come eat breakfast with him.

"You just want me to make your breakfast," Franci said.

"If you don't, you can't wear my shirt."

"You have to drive us, you know."

Lucas sat cross-legged on the bed and fingered through his mother's jewelry box. He lingered, hoping she might change her mind about taking him. Lucas had large grey eyes. His hair fell evenly, like a bowl around his head, and his cheeks looked as though someone had smeared dark rouge on them. They were more than a healthy color, they were impossible not to notice. And anyone who met him commented on his cheeks. They spoke as though they couldn't figure them out.

He picked up a strand of pearls and some cheap earrings. "Are these expensive?" he asked.

"Very," she said. "Put those back." He loved the thought that he was handling her most expensive things.

The kitchen looked like a cage at the zoo: a cereal bowl spilled, PopTarts half-eaten, an attempt at some eggs, a spoon flung under the toaster, milk out, and three half-glasses of orange Gatorade in the sink.

"Did you eat breakfast?" Molly called to no one in particular. No one answered her. They were already in Joe's car. Molly took Franci's lunch out to her. Lucas sat lodged between Joe and Franci and had his books on his lap. The window stayed down for only a few seconds, so that Franci's hair would not be long-exposed to the morning air. Molly kissed her, but didn't touch her hair.

"I'll call tonight," Molly promised, though no one seemed to care about that particular promise.

"Will you bring back whatever Papa Frank sends me?" Franci said.

"Well, he might not . . ." She stopped herself. "I'll bring it." She told Joe goodbye. He looked tall, even sitting in the car. His arms had a warm, tensile strength. Lucas didn't kiss her goodbye. He wore a dirty shirt and wouldn't look at anyone, only at his books that lay stacked neatly on his lap, his hands draped over them, like a fish. The car window framed them in a wide glass picture, and their faces carried like different flags all the desires not yet answered by their hearts.

Before William left the house, he kissed Molly quickly on the cheek.

"Give your father my love," he said. It seemed a strange thing to say, and his expression said he knew it was odd. "I'll take care of everything here. Don't worry." She didn't know what he was waiting for.

"I won't."

The phone rang as William pulled out of the driveway. It was Asa Caldwell.

"I have some room for a few paintings, if you have anything ready," he said. Asa was the curator at the museum in Asheville. He had placed Molly's first paintings and since then tried to keep her work before the public. He put them in a room of Local Artists. She had three drawings, she said.

"But they're all done in pencil and white paint. They look so spare, I can hardly believe they're my own." She'd spent each morning for the past few months working separately on these white pages. When Will went to work and the children to school, she let the weight of herself spread through these lines. She had not always painted, though she had, for as long as she could remember, found her understanding of the world through an image, or an array of lines and pattern that kept repeating itself. She knew what these things were to her, but she never could judge whether or not they would sell.

"I'll look at them," Asa said.

"They might not be what you want." Molly always said this to protect herself. She wrapped up the drawings and, as she did, saw all she had done that was wrong. "He will hate these," she said out loud.

Most of the lines did not meet, but just missed meeting, and in that missing she had created a form that was recognizably human. The penciled lines gave a soft, human component to the interval of white-painted ground. If she stood back, stepped a few feet from the drawing, it seemed she was looking at someone through a big white sheet.

Just as she was about to go out the door, William called from the office. He asked if she had cashed a check yet for this week. Molly told him the money was in the second drawer of the kitchen desk.

"Good," he said. "Well."

"Okay." She put the phone down on its cradle, soundlessly, like an eyelid closing, and she wondered if William walked into the house right now, would he even recognize who she was.

If you saw Stringer's Ridge from the air, if you saw the town, you would see how the houses themselves formed a circle around a fragment of the French Broad River. Houses began to sprout two miles from the river, and forests made the whole town flush with new green. If you came nearer you would hear birds in abundant droves, and at this time of year the jonquils and tulips were in full bloom and dogwood buds large. Blunt, fat-bodied swifts moved around in ragtag fashion and rumors of bluebirds were passed from house to house. People in Stringer's Ridge were interested in such things, and since the town was closed in on all sides by mountains, they had a conscious faith in themselves. They looked rested and powerless. They looked as though they were always teasing you.

The first time William and Molly drove through Stringer's Ridge, Joe was four and Franci only a few months old. The main difference in William and Molly then and now was that the years had made them tense. William's work was only beginning to be recognized and he did not yet know the pressure of keeping up with the pace he had set for himself. He had won an award for artistic design on a building in a suburb of Asheville, and from that came a job with a firm there. After years of success, Will began to drink cups of coffee with more sugar and less milk, and sometimes after supper he slept on the couch. He began working at home. Molly was tired all the time, and they never talked to each other.

But at this early time when they came to Asheville and drove through Stringer's Ridge, they were both doing what they wanted to do, and when Molly saw a house for sale, she suggested they look at it.

The two-story house sat at the edge of town. It had more rooms than they needed, but they could see the creek and the French Broad River from the upstairs windows. Molly's eyes still grew rested every time she looked out from her bedroom. There were cathedral windows and arched doorways. The backyard had a weeping cherry tree and a broken-down gazebo in the far corner of the lot. The gazebo was draped with wisteria, and when it was thick with blooms, looked more snakey than lovely.

There was a basement which they decided could be turned into a playroom, but they never did so. Joe and Franci used the basement to frighten Lucas. They described ghostly figures who lived behind the water heater, and they dressed him in what they called "protective clothing": Will's blue jacket, red socks, and a hairnet worn by women at the Waffle Shoppe. They held a ritual rehearsal, then sent Lucas downstairs and closed the door. They said he had to.

Joe and Franci explained how they, too, had gone through the ritual several years earlier, and look how it had saved them. If Lucas refused to do this, his room might be haunted on certain nights (though not every night). It was up to him, they said. Lucas endured the ritual partly because he was afraid not to and partly because his wish to be included was stronger than his fear.

They had lived in this house for twelve years now. It was the only home Lucas and Franci had ever known, and the only one Joe had ever cared about.

Asa liked the pencil-and-white drawings. He said he could see the natural ring of people. No one touching. He said that each component worked like an instrument, or model, of companionship. Molly didn't know what he meant when he talked about her work. But when she left the gallery after hearing his comments, she felt the calm detachment of success.

The mountains of North Carolina unraveled into open fields and mossy trees as she drove toward Savannah. It was a sunny afternoon. Molly could never paint the sunshine on a landscape. She never got right the brightness against the shadow. Once, she almost found the right pattern when she painted an iron gate. In her own mind it was the closest she had come, but Asa never took that one.

As the afternoon wore on, the sun thinned behind the trees and Molly trembled in anticipation of her father's loneliness. She searched for familiar landmarks—graveyards, a huge water tower built to look like a peach, a deserted churchhouse that marked her midway point, and then two miles from the church, a sign that read: Bolied PeaNuts.

The dogwoods this far south were in full bloom. They were in full bloom last year when her mother was sick, and she knew her father thought of this. Molly felt stabbed by the sight of Savannah in the distance—the fat trees, the moss, the swampy places. Everything here delighted in its own privacy.

Molly hadn't mentioned to her father anything about her trouble with William. She told Jill, because she told Jill everything and because Jill asked her in particular frankness, "What's going on with you two? You act like you can't stand each other anymore." But besides Jill, Molly hadn't told a soul.

She ate the apple and cookies as she got hungry, and waited until afternoon to eat her sandwich. At three-thirty she stopped at a small, dark store that said GROC. and bought a cup of strong coffee and some crackers. She sat in the sunshine on a bench outside the store. The bench looked more like a pew. Two men came outside and stood around the gas pumps while she ate.

One man was fat and bald. He stood barricaded behind reflector sunglasses and a cap. The other was younger and carried a Sprite he kept drinking from, even though there was none left in the bottle. The men knew each other and talked back and forth, but their talk was mostly for Molly. They wore greasy pants and shoes, and Molly tried to picture them as little boys with young hands and faces, or as young men, slamming doors. She could see a trace of handsomeness in one and knew he still thought of himself as desirable.

Finally the Sprite-man walked over to Molly. "I seen you here before," he said. Molly didn't speak. "You been here. Before."

Molly had always received this kind of attention. She didn't mind it, but she didn't feel flattered by it anymore. "I was here two months ago," she said. The younger man hit the other one's arm. "I told you I seen her. It was two months ago." He said this as though he hadn't heard Molly just say it. "And you had somebody with you."

"No," Molly said. She told them her father lived in Savannah.

"I got a aunt lives there. She's dead now though. Cecie Powers. You know her?"

Molly shook her head. She wanted to leave. "Well," she said, standing. The other man studied her, and she hoped he wouldn't speak.

"You from there?" the other man said. His voice was low and gravelly, as though he had been sick.

"Since I was nine," Molly said. She threw away the rest of her crackers, and drank down to the dregs of the coffee. She wanted to spit it out, but didn't. She said she had to go and made a comment about being late. She pretended to hurry. Both men watched as she drove off. She saw them sit on the bench pew and kept in mind the order they presented in her rearview mirror. She imagined they sat there every day, and that her presence had been an intrusion they wanted.

"I don't love you" kept coming into Molly's mind. "Anymore" came in separately sometimes. Just that word alone, like the refrain of a song that makes you think of the whole thing, the refrain played in so many ways: Lucas clearing his throat and Molly knowing this might be the beginning of a nervous habit. Clearing it without needing to, without even talking.

"Honey?"

"What?" Throat cleared.

"You hungry?"

Cleared. "For what?"

"Ice cream?"

"Yeah." Cleared.

If Molly lived to be a hundred, nobody could accuse her in a more specific way.

The landscape as she came close to Savannah included broken lines and debris, desperate shacks with swept yards, and usually a large tree near a house. Molly could smell the swampy marshes, and she felt reformed. The countenance of elms in the water and the smell of animals were what she remembered of swamp. Black sod and the sea nearby—a double harness thrown around her.

As she came to Savannah's city limits the light grew more saffron. Noises came out of the ground the way they had when she was a child. Crepuscular insects and this enfeebled light made her try to picture the way her father looked then.

Frank Bates was not old yet, but the sway of his back was getting old. The first time Molly thought of his oldness was when she walked behind him into the swamp. She had been to the swamp many times with her cousin during summer months, but her father thought this was her first time, so she pretended she had never been before. She felt superior pretending. She saw his oldness in the way he bent down or squinted into the nest of squirrels. He told some old story about the swamp. Molly had heard it before but listened appreciatively. She could not tell him she had heard it, would never tell him such a thing.

As she drove onto Savannah's streets, she scrutinized the road and could see the radio station, but someone had turned the building into an auto parts place because on the window was painted: Jader's Parts and Auto Supply.

The radio station used to be the landmark that meant you were entering town from the north side. Molly felt adventurous seeing it, because her mother had told her never to go past it, never to go as far as that. So Molly had seen it as an end point. Sometimes she had tried to imagine what was beyond it.

As she turned down West Glen Road, she saw her father's house. The yard beside the house had grown too high. There had been several families to live next door to Frank Bates, the last a divorced man and his son. Molly wondered if she would ever be divorced.

All of this went through her mind, and the wind blew a strict breeze through the tops of trees. Then she saw her father in the driveway. He looked like the same shadowy figure who would wait for her when she returned home from dates with William.

Frank Bates was a large man, his hair whiter than a year ago but still thick, and his hands looked more like the hands of a day laborer than a newspaperman. He wore a blue chambray button-down shirt, very expensive. Molly knew he had bought it for her visit. He wanted her to think he was doing fine, and was embarrassed now that he had asked her to come here.

Molly got out of the car and went toward him. It was dark and the light behind him kept her from seeing his face. She tried to picture him as a boy, but even though she had heard remote fictions of his early years, she couldn't picture him any way but what he was now.

She knew she had his coloring and his eyes, his deep forehead. She knew she had her mother's hair and nose. Her mouth was no one's but her own. It was too large for her face. William said it was the kind of mouth men liked. William had always commented on Molly's mouth.

Frank Bates greeted Molly with an open look of appreciation and a long kiss on the cheek. "I feel very deceptive," he said.

"Why?"

"I'm not as sad as I sounded on the phone." He led her into the kitchen, where dinner was ready. He had prepared chicken, peas, and rice, the way her mother would have done. Each item was lined up in bowls on the counter. Everything was cold, but he hadn't thought of that.

"I think maybe you are." Molly served their plates from the bowls. The table was set with her mother's placemats and yellow napkins. The forks sat on the wrong side of the plates.

"I haven't felt sad today." He spoke with caution and a fantastic anxiety. "I've been going through her things all day and haven't felt the way I expected to feel. I shouldn't have pulled you away from your family."

"You didn't pull me away."

"Still."

"I think you are sad," she told him again, "but I don't think you're sad all the time. You don't have to be miserable every minute in order to ask me to come here."

Frank laughed. "Okay." He had brought the bowls to the table, and Molly took another helping of rice. Frank poured tea for Molly and milk for himself. "It's acidophilus," he said as though he knew something Molly didn't. "I started drinking it at night instead of tea." He sat upright as he told her this, and Molly was glad for the development of a new pattern in his life. She was trying to discover new patterns for herself.

"How's Will?" he asked.

"Fine." Molly gave an obligatory smile, learned in childhood. She said how he was working on plans for a new building in Asheville. She did not say how his last few clients were displeased with his work and that for the past two years he had been in a slump. "He's always busy," she said. Then she reached into her purse and took out Franci's quotes. She read them aloud to her father as he ate, and Frank Bates appeared to enjoy them with a secret pleasure that ran between himself and Franci. Both of them, though, were aware that Molly had changed the subject.

They exchanged smiles, covert and full of relief. They were both swimming upstream and they liked the company of each other. But the act of swimming was separate and both knew it.

He pulled a paper from his shirt pocket and Molly thought it would be a response to Franci's quotes. He had something to tell her, he said, and he blossomed into his childhood face. It was Molly's first look at him with the years shed away. He brought out a letter which he obviously thought they had discussed. "These are the people I told you about." Molly did not say he had failed to mention it.

The people were Louise and Sig Penry, a couple who lived in Shelby, North Carolina. Frank wanted Molly to stop by their house on her way home. Molly did not want to. She said she had never heard of them.

"I know I mentioned them to you," Frank protested. They washed dishes together and put them away. Molly read the Penrys' letter and asked about Frank's plans. She decided that maybe he had been deceptive, that maybe this was the reason he wanted her to visit, rather than to work in the attic.

"I'm writing an article about them, something that might be syndicated. I've done the research already. They use their home as a place for abused children and they've even kept several of the kids for five or six years. Raised them themselves. They've been doing this for almost a decade, and now the state says they're not legal."

"How did you hear about it?"

"Somebody put a note and an article from the Shelby paper on my desk. I wrote to the Penrys and we've been corresponding for several months."

All of this seemed extreme to Molly. She wanted to warn her father, but couldn't think of what warning to give.

"If I stop there on my way back, what do you want me to do?"

"Just meet them. Tell me what you see. I'll have to make the trip myself pretty soon, but I'd like to have your impression." He looked at Molly thoughtfully.

"I could do that," Molly agreed. She spoke as though she thought it was going to be simple.

Molly had forgotten to call home. She said she would do so now.

"Lucas? Is that you?"

"Yeah. Hey."

"Everything all right?"

"Yeah. Grey cat is sick." The cat weighed fifteen pounds and they called him Grey because they could never agree on a name. The name was supposed to be temporary.

"What do you mean?"

"He vomits all the time. He did it on your bed. Dad threw him out the window, because he didn't see the vomit until he sat on the bed and got it on him."

"Where is he now?"

"He ran under the house."

"No, I mean where is *Dad*?"

"He called and said for us to order pizza. He won't be home till ten."

"Mom?" Franci had picked up the other phone. "The cat got sick."

"I know. Lucas told me."

"You should've seen Dad. It was hy*ster*ical."

"Where's Joe?"

"He went to get the pizza. He wouldn't let us go with him."

"Do you have any homework?"

"I've already done it. Lucas hadn't even *started* his."

"I don't *have* any."

"I want you to be sure to leave some pizza for your dad," Molly said, "and don't give any to the cat."

"When'll you be home?" Lucas asked.

"In a few days."

"Did you give Papa Frank our presents?"

"I was just about to," she said.

"Mama, when are you coming home?" Franci made her voice sound like an unclaimed possession. "Everything is so *hard*."

Franci exaggerated, but she always understood things intuitively, before she knew them in her mind. Two days ago when Molly woke, Franci was standing over her. Franci had walked in her sleep again, but didn't remember where she was. Molly scooted closer to William and Franci got in beside her. They dozed for thirty more minutes, until the sky was the color of pink hydrangeas.

When Papa Frank opened the Redskins shirt, he laughed with such fondness that Molly wished she had brought Lucas with her. When he saw Franci's coin, a light came to his face and he said, "Franci is so much like your mother. Do you know that?" Molly said she knew it, but what she wanted to hear was that Franci was like herself.

They watched the last part of a spy movie, and Molly guessed the ending. When it was over, neither of them was ready to go to bed, so Frank got out a deck of cards.

"Poker?" He had taught Molly and Robby to play poker during the summer Molly was eleven. Robby was the cousin who spent most summers with them, and they had played poker every night, for toothpicks.

That was the same summer Frank Bates put them to bed (even though they were both too old for it) and told them jokes. Molly and Robby never understood the jokes. And later, when they got older and did understand them, they knew they weren't funny. Frank Bates never told jokes in public, because Evelyn had said he didn't tell them right. In a social gathering Evelyn Bates told jokes for him. He allowed this, because she could make people laugh. But Molly felt sorry when her father's joke was taken away, so she told Robby to always laugh when he got to the end of a joke. "When is the end?" Robby asked. "Just watch when I laugh," Molly said. And her father's joy at making them laugh was sealed that summer.

They played poker for almost an hour, then Frank Bates said, "You look tired." He said it the way people who are tired say it to people who aren't. He got up to go to bed.

"Goodnight," he said.

Last year, when the three of them were together and they had prepared a room for Evelyn to die in, he'd carried Evelyn back to her room each night. "You are so much trouble," he'd say, pretending she was a burden.

"You don't have to carry me. I can walk." Evelyn barely could walk most days.

"If you were as fat as you used to be, I wouldn't be able to hold you with these old arms."

"You aren't old," she told him, "just weak." She laughed and they looked like lovers. "I'm too thin. You liked me fat."

"You look good to me. You look fine." He kissed her cheek and Molly walked behind them to the back room. Molly had imagined this might be similar to the way they talked before making love. It seemed as intimate as that.

Molly would sleep in her mother's room. She turned down the covers. Her father had put on clean sheets, but the bed, the whole room, had the faint smell of powder.

She slipped between the sheets and thought of the constellations beyond this room. She wanted to bring order to her mind. The astronomy course she was taking now had introduced her to a more natural order. The movements of the planets and stars went through her like a visible stream, and whenever she thought of these things she could sleep.

Last spring, she had slept on a cot beside this bed, close enough to minister to her mother's hard needs. She had wanted to push her mother's face into the fullness of health, to sculpt it away from the slackness of chin and forehead and bring it back to a rosy color. The balance of nose and mouth was wrong, not anything familiar. But Molly couldn't change what her mother had become. She could not force a structure different from the one the disease had already sculpted.

In spending years looking at your children, bathing them, knowing their frightened eyes and the nervousness that comes into their hands and feet, knowing them in all the ways—the color of their urine, their stools, the rash and how it looks each hour—after knowing that, there is never any way of "unknowing" them or treating them as though you do not know these things. But you never expect to know a parent like that, and the parent never expects it either. How strange to know the lineaments and features of a mother's body and back, the geographical wounds, the aging skin like some history report.

One night Molly soaked a rag in cool alcohol to give her mother a rubdown the way the nurses had instructed. She turned Evelyn over in one soft move and washed her old belly. It was a shocking thing to do. But for a few days afterwards, her mother got back some of her old vigor and Frank Bates had the face of someone who believed in miracles. "Maybe she's going to be all right," he had said.

Molly woke early the next day to walk on the beach. The wind blew clouds and changed the way the sand looked. The temperature in Savannah was ten degrees warmer than in Stringer's Ridge, and the air shivered and bloomed and had the smell of summer about to begin.

She had brought two cinnamon rolls from the pantry. They were stale. She would eat them anyway. She ate one, and broke off pieces from the other to feed the gulls. She sat awhile, imagining Franci and Lucas getting ready for school. She hoped Will had made their lunches. Joe would have to drive them again.

Whenever things weren't going well, her mother had taught Molly to name two good things that had happened. One was that Asa was considering her paintings; the other was that Franci made an A on her math test. Another good thing was how well her father was surviving.

She wanted to tell her father about Will, how their whole house had the weight of some unspeakable crime, how she felt the shame of failure. But she couldn't tell him that.

The time she mentioned it to Jill, even then, she stated what she had to say with the glibness of everything being only momentarily unbalanced.

"You know how he gets," Molly said, "when his work's not going right. I think that's it." She knew it wasn't, and Jill did too, but Jill wouldn't pretend with Molly.

"Molly." She didn't know how much to say. "I'm not so sure it's just a mood."

"I didn't say that."

"It's what you meant."

"I know it's not a mood. I know he's getting ready to leave."

"So think of what to do. Think what you'll do next."

"I don't know."

"You don't believe what you just said then."

"No. I don't."

"Okay." Jill was conscious of words being a block between them. "Let's go eat." Neither mentioned it the rest of that day.

When Molly got back to the house, her father was reading on the porch. He said he was ready to work in the attic if she was.

"Is something wrong?" He looked up from the book to see that he had turned a corner into her privacy, a shift in the course of boundaries.

Her blood slowed. "What do you mean?"

"It's you and Will, isn't it? That's what's wrong." She didn't know what she had done to let him see this in her.

"I don't want to talk about it."

If her mother had dreams, Molly never knew what they were, but her father wore his dreams on his sleeve. He championed causes and fell on the sword for helpless people. He lived in the inexorable clutter of what others only worried about. His dreams were heroic and impossible, though sometimes he made them come true. He didn't become immobilized by paradox, and Molly hoped she had some of his courage inside herself.

The attic was hot. She could smell the odor of him, but saw only the top of his head over the boxes. For a split second both her mother and father seemed reduced to a hodgepodge of boxes. She began to clear out the first pile of clothes, her mother's dresses and hats. Some of the hats had wide-holed net.

"Molly. Listen to this." He motioned with his hand and held up a note. It was not written to him, but he read portions of it aloud. It was written to her mother from a man named Jeff Foster.

"You remember him?"

Molly didn't remember him at all. "I think I do."

Frank read something else, another note. This one implicated both her mother and Jeff Foster.

"I don't want to hear this," Molly said. To be curious about it seemed unfair. "I mean it." She became irritated. He seemed to be going through everything with the slowness of a convalescent walking down a long hall. This whole process involved a more than considerable translation. Molly began to think of her father as weak and old, but she hated what she thought.

One of the neighbor's dogs had got loose and was chasing a cat, or a truck, with a vow to tear apart whichever it was. When the dog stopped barking, the quietness left the impression of turmoil.

"Why are you telling me this?"

"I want you to talk to me."

"But it's not like that. That's not it." Molly felt unyielding toward her own and Will's defense.

"What is it then? It'd be better if you would name it." Then Frank Bates spoke in the tone of a patronizing older figure. "These things happen in a marriage." He was guessing.

But he couldn't divert Molly into any conversation, for relief or for uproar. Molly said she would work alone for a while. Nothing was complete between them. Later, after dinner, Frank suggested that Molly look up old friends while she was here. Molly said she would.

The next day they worked without incident and Molly saw two friends who came by the house. They stayed until past suppertime. After they left, her father asked again if she would stop in Shelby to see the Penrys. He took out a map and pointed to the place he thought they lived.

"It's a farm," he said. "About here, I think."

"What should I say to them?"

Frank made a list of questions for Molly to ask, and the change from irritation to camaraderie was intoxicating. They'd finished most of the attic work, and Molly called Will to say she would be home tomorrow.

"Is your father all right?" His affection for her father was genuine.

"He's fine." Molly spoke to Lucas on the extension and said that Papa Frank might come for a visit at the end of April.

William was so quiet when she said this that there was no mistaking his plans. He was so quiet that Molly thought he was off the phone until he spoke.

"I'll tell the kids you'll be here tomorrow."

"Late," she said. "Tell Lucas." Lucas had hung up the extension. "Tell him he can wait up."

There was a moment when no one said anything, then William said, "Your astronomy professor called." His words were clipped and idle. "I didn't talk to him, but the kids said he called. He wanted to know if you were sick."

Molly laughed. "I haven't missed one class, not one," she explained, because William seemed to be asking for an explanation. "I guess he was surprised. I had a presentation to make and forgot to call and say I wouldn't be there." All of this was true, but sounded like a made-up excuse, or a lie.

"Well, anyway," said William, "he called."

CHAPTER
TWO

It was true that Molly hadn't missed one class. In fact, she stayed late several times to discuss what the subject of her report should be. Her astronomy notes were full of ideas, but nothing that focused her attention. She asked Professor McGinnis to help her decide on a topic, and she even brought her notes for him to see.

She hesitated in handing over her notebook, because so much subjective material lay woven into the facts. Before she handed it to him, she explained that she was a painter, not a scientist, and that these physical structures and their patterns seemed similar to human relationships. She said the way these things worked helped her to understand connections between humans and the world. "Anyway," she said, so he would know she meant all of this as an apology.

"That's interesting." He spoke sincerely. "I like that idea." He looked at her first page of notes.

January 18, 1986

The earth is boundless, but not infinite. Because of its curvature, we return to the point of departure.

Einstein—Behind the quantum fuzziness and disorder lies a world
of concrete reality. Movement and happenings are in accordance
with laws of cause and effect. This "madhouse of paradox is a fa-
cade"—at the deeper level is sanity.

I look for corollaries.

Once, as a child, I saw blind people in a community outside Savannah. They made colorful baskets and quilts. Some made pottery—
vases, cups, bowls. Patterns and colors made (though not seen) by
these people. Many had been blind since birth. Others remembered,
so when I described their own work to them, they smiled. They knew
what I meant. The eyes of a few were white. I couldn't look into their
faces.

January 26, 1986

David Bohm—Qualitative and quantitative differences: In a sandbox are infinite numbers of ways to arrange grains of sand (quantitative), but it has one quality—that of being a sandbox (qualitative).
When children play in the sandbox, interacting with the sand, it ac-
quires new qualities.

Idea for painting: Children in a sandbox. Wintertime. They wear
coats. Sun comes through the trees—harsh, wintry. Sand is spilling
around the sides of the box. Children are different ages. They are at
different stages of concentration. The space between them must—
and their gestures must—put in mind a force acting between them.

Look up binary star systems.

"All these things come together in my mind," Molly said, still
apologizing for the mixture of facts and life.

Professor McGinnis looked through several pages of notes and
suggested two things. One, that they talk about her project at the
coffee shop down the street, and two, that she call him Ben instead
of Professor McGinnis. They were the same age after all, he said. He
made both suggestions sound harmless.

Ben McGinnis was taller than Will. He had been divorced for six
years and had the look of someone who knew how to be alone.

They walked to the coffee shop and he said that if she didn't mind he would order something to eat. He hadn't had dinner yet. Molly ordered coffee and said she would like some of the good homemade rolls they baked here.

"I've never been divorced," she said stupidly when he mentioned how long he had lived alone.

"I know."

The waitress brought him a small steak smothered in mushrooms, mashed potatoes. He offered Molly the basket of rolls. His shirt was open at the neck, no tie. She could see the dark hair on his chest. He opened the napkin that covered the bread. His arm came toward her. His hand near her face, his wristbone exposed at the sleeve, the warm bread smell—these things, and the way he did them, made Molly want to take off all her clothes.

"How is Will?" her father asked.

"He said my astronomy professor called," Molly explained. "I was supposed to give a report this week and forgot to say I wouldn't be there."

"What was the report about?" Frank Bates was careful to ask the right thing. She told him the report was on precession, and she began to explain it to him.

"I know about precession of planets."

"You do?"

He thought she was teasing him. "Don't you remember how I took you and Robby out on summer nights and we lay in the grass and named the constellations? Vega and the Summer Triangle? Remember that?"

"There's another precession besides the planets."

"Tell me something new, daughter."

"It's the same precession, it's all the same. It's a wobble that occurs when the earth spins, like a top winding down, so the positions of the stars change as the earth's axis changes its spin. And that makes for a leisurely difference in the way we see a star over a period of years, and sometimes the planets too. Sometimes it makes the planets look like they're traveling backwards. For a while people thought they were, but it was only the way things looked."

"Did you put all this in your report?"

Molly described to him the graphs and pictures she had included.

"Professor McGinnis. What's he like?"

"He's very patient with my ideas. We've had coffee a couple of times." It had been three times.

Her father wore a look of distrust, and she wanted to say: Nothing happened. Nothing at all happened, but she wasn't sure this was true. She wanted to say how Will no longer loved her, but she didn't know if that was true either.

"I don't know, Molly."

Molly felt his blame.

"I'm not my mother," she said.

Molly stood and took her cup and spoon to the sink. "I want to get an early start in the morning." But Frank Bates could not let her leave this way. He moved behind her at the sink and held her close for a long moment. Molly didn't know how long it had been since she had been held this way. A massive concurrence of forces worked inside her. When he let her go, her hands fumbled with the cup and the spoon she had laid down so judiciously.

When she arrived three days ago, her father took the trouble to prepare dinner and Molly felt protected by his care; now his protection had turned to assault and back again to care. This kind of change can happen so easily with fathers, and sometimes there is no visible event to name where it all turned.

She had not been on the road for more than a few hours when she heard the forecast of a storm. Warnings first, then mention of a tornado watch. As Molly crossed the North Carolina line, one forecaster grew more intense, saying that tornadoes had already been sighted in several counties. Molly pulled off at the next truck stop to get more information.

"Some of the farms are already tore up bad." One trucker sat at the counter and heard Molly ask about the roads. "It's headed straight this way too." He had enormous arms and a stout neck, and even though he directed his words to the waitress, he was speaking to Molly. He looked straight at her. "You better come on and go with me, little lady." He laughed loudly to let everyone know he had said something clever.

Molly asked if anyone knew Sig and Louise Penry, and how far from here they lived. The waitress knew. "Near Shelby," she said. "You can almost see their house from the interstate."

The truck driver stood up and said his name. The way his arms stuck out he looked like a stuffed bear, and he extended one hand toward Molly. Molly did not think of him as attractive, but as she walked to her car she imagined that he loved her.

She drove toward the mountains, and the sky changed. Wind pulled at the trees and the air turned dark and green. Clouds grew thick, as the sky took on the face of a sullen child.

The waitress had told Molly to look for a storage building on the left, "then take the first exit after that." Molly saw it and pulled off at the exit. She could see the top of a farmhouse.

The road that led to the house was dirt. Molly caught a glint of reflection from the doorway and could see a woman in the yard taking sheets off the line. She left her car and went toward the woman.

Pellets of ice the size of marbles bounced off the hood of the car, and in only a short time the ground was covered with the hard pieces. The screen door at the side of the house banged open and shut, and Molly heard a man calling to someone inside. Beyond the field she could see a cloud shaped like a large spoon forming itself on a hill. The sky around it was pink and bruised, and the air had the peculiar smell of copper.

When the rain came, it was as though it came from someplace other than the sky. It blew in gusts, as dust does, or sand. The woman hurried to the house with sheets bundled under her arms. When she saw Molly, she motioned for her to go into the house. Molly stepped into their kitchen to see a man opening windows in another room.

"Bring the lantern," he said. He didn't speak to Molly, but to the small boy beside him. The boy, about five, lifted the lantern, as the man got blankets and a jug of water. The woman brought pillows and they headed out the back door toward an old silo forty yards from the house. The noise of the wind was so loud now, they had to shout to be heard.

The silo was a grain shaft that hadn't been used for years. Molly could see that part of the shaft went at least ten feet into the ground, and there was a small, odd-shaped room where the mechanism which operated the grain elevator had been and where they would go now. The leg of the elevator was still there.

The shaft lay slanted, so that as they climbed down into it each person had to incline himself to the slant. Molly wedged herself next to the man, the boy lay flat, and the woman scooted down beside them. The woman was not as fat as she appeared at first. They closed themselves in by pulling a flat door over the top of the shaft, and the boy lit the lantern as though he had been told exactly what to do.

"Sig, I brought these pillows for your back." The woman spoke first. She stuffed two pillows behind Sig, then turned to hand Molly the water jug. "We won't be here long," she said. She had done this before, and it felt safe when she spoke. It felt safe because of the woman, and because of the slant and the way they all inclined themselves toward it.

Every time something hit against the metal top of the shaft, everyone ducked, though there was no need to do so. The thickness of the shaft lining held them safe inside and though the lantern flickered briefly a few times, it didn't go all the way out. Their bright forms were to Molly an intaglio reflecting underground—like fish in deep water when the daylight reaches a depth and gives the forms it hits a moment of literal quaking.

"I forgot to bring . . ." the boy started, but the man made him be quiet. "What's it doing?" He wanted to talk.

There were noises, but the crashing they heard died down and Sig told everyone it had not come too close. "Louise," he said after a little while, "lift it up," and Louise lifted the makeshift door so they could crawl out.

The silo was intact and so was the house, but the damage done to the field and woods made the ground appear changed, sagged. It had the look of something that had been long forgotten.

The screen door Molly had opened a short while ago was blown off its hinges and lay in the yard. The clothesline was nowhere to be seen, and as they went inside the house they could hear glass breaking somewhere upstairs. Each person stood as if he were alone, and what Molly noticed first was how many pictures there were. Some still hung on the wall, but most were strewn over the floor, both separate and in frames.

When they said their names, Louise and Sig said theirs first and introduced Tony. They said he was not their own. Molly told them she was Frank Bates' daughter. Louise clapped her hands together once, and Sig expanded his chest with hope. These people were like subjects of a poem—simple hands and faces, their bodies indistinct except for Sig's square size.

Louise began the work of straightening the house. She told Tony to pick up the pictures. They lay everywhere—single shots, groups, all of them hapless children and all different ages.

A limb had crushed the back end of Molly's car, but Sig said he could pull it off with his tractor. He left for the barn and Tony ran to go with him.

"I dreamed of this," said Louise, forgetting about everything but what Frank Bates could do and the fact that Molly was here. "I hoped somebody might be interested enough to take us on."

"Well, I don't know," said Molly. She didn't want to offer much hope. "I don't know what he's thinking, but he asked me to come by and meet you." Molly needed to call home. She could get the operator, but lines were down and her call couldn't go through.

It was late in the afternoon before the limb was pulled off the car, the pictures back in their frames, and the telephone lines working again. Molly and Louise had talked, and when Molly remembered to take out the questions her father had written down, she found that there was no need to ask anything else. Louise told her more than the questions asked.

"When I married Sig, my family almost disowned me. They said he wouldn't ever have money, but they didn't know Sig. Then after we'd been married a few years some cousin left him a big inheritance. Sig didn't even know this cousin had money." Louise laughed. "We'd already started taking in children by that time, but the money meant we could take in more. And Sig built the place in back." She pointed to a dormitory-like building behind the house. "We've had as many as twenty-five to thirty here at a time. And when people find out what we're doing, they bring food and clothes and some give money. That's how the county heard about it." She spoke of "the county" as though it were someone candidly stupid.

"They came out and told us none of this was legal, especially the way we took in money." She laughed again. "So we're thinking of what to do. Your father suggested we get a lawyer and we have one, but I think he's not big enough to win something like this. Sig says to let the public know about it. Get the public on our side."

The county had taken away many of Louise and Sig's children and placed them in an old hotel that served as a home. It was dreary, Louise said, "not at all like this place."

Louise's hair was full of grey, with a darker streak of iron-grey that went down one side. Her skin spread on her face like thin clear paper, and her eyes—a startling splash of blue. She spoke out the window now to Sig, but it was Tony who answered. Tony followed Sig everywhere he went.

The afternoon light lay like a scrap of nylon on the torn-up fields. It was almost four o'clock, and the car wasn't ready yet. Round-eyed Louise had exposed her invisible threads of passion without knowing it, and Molly felt tied to the lives of people whose names she had never heard until a few days ago.

"Where are you?" Joe answered the phone when she called.

"Outside Shelby."

"There was a tornado."

"I know."

"Were you in it?" Franci was on the other phone.

"Yes. I'll tell you all about it."

"Ga!" Lucas had taken the phone from Franci. Molly heard them argue over it.

"Dad's home," Franci said, assuming her mother would want to speak to him.

"Molly?" His voice was quick, urgent even. "Where are you?"

"I'm fine," she said.

"We were worried," Will said. "News of the storm was on TV. Your father called."

"I'll be home later tonight."

"Can I stay up till you get here?" Franci asked. "Even if it's late?" She wanted to see her mother.

"Yes."

"Ga! Can I?"

Molly got home at nine-thirty. She told them about the silo and Louise and Sig. She made the storm sound worse than it was, and Franci and Lucas listened with the attention of someone waiting to be introduced.

"Were you scared?" Franci's dark eyes and forehead were William's, but she had her mother's wide mouth and her own textural, numbered way of looking at the world. "*I* would've been scared." She had taken a bath and her cheeks looked smooth as riverstones. Her face and arms flushed with a waxy, warm dignity.

"Not so much."

William sat on the sofa beside Molly. His clothes and hair did not rest on him in the usual way. They appeared amok. Once when Molly looked at him she thought she caught an expression of complicity, and she told everything with more excitement to see if she could raise the stakes.

She talked both of the storm and of Louise and Sig. The storm now seemed nothing compared to the open and crashing way Louise wished for things. Molly knew how that wishing, when it goes on for a long time, is like magic. That kind of wishing, even if nothing comes from it, turns into hope. And Louise's face bloomed so full that it seemed anyone around her was wearing a mask.

She put Lucas to bed and he asked about Papa Frank, but Franci still wanted to know if her mother had been afraid, and she wouldn't believe anything until Molly said, "I guess I was pretty scared, Franci. I guess you're right." So Franci went to sleep. Her arms and legs stuck out from the covers, and her body held its energy like wild fruit.

The first sound they heard the next morning was Jill knocking on the door. She would be late to work, she said, but wanted to make sure Molly was home. Jill Corcoran had been Molly's best friend for ten years.

"You could've called me last night!"

"It was late."

"I came over twice to check on this crew." She pointed to Franci and Lucas.

"She took us to get ice cream."

"Gelato!" said Franci, to show she remembered what Jill had taught them.

"Tastes like ice cream to me."

Jill had a rather undistinguished beauty, but made up for it with clothes that clashed in color, and an almost punk hairdo. She was thirty-eight, and though she hadn't always been single, she'd been single as long as Molly had known her. She was a photographer for the daily paper and did some freelance work for magazines.

She wanted to ask about William, but waited until the children went to school. "Will's not here?"

"He left early."

"What's going on?" Jill sat down. She wanted to find out something.

"I swear I don't know. He seemed so nice last night. Like he cared, or was worried about me because of the storm."

"You have to be careful, Molly." Jill had been involved with a man for almost a year now, and she seemed to be talking about herself.

"Careful about what? What should I be careful about?"

"About messing up your life!"

It was apparent that Jill had an agenda in mind, but she hadn't told Molly yet. "Jill, what are you talking about?"

"Nothing," she said. "I'm just mad because you haven't called in two weeks. How is your dad?" She liked Frank Bates, and they talked newspaper whenever he came to town.

"He could tell something was wrong with me and Will. I didn't tell him. He just knew."

"Sometimes," Jill said, "I think everybody knows everything, but we just walk around acting like we don't. It's easier." She said she had to go to work. "I'm late. Listen," she said, "I want you to cut my hair."

"Okay, but I won't know what to cut. It's so short now."

"No. I mean I want something more traditional. Short and easy, not wild."

"What's this man doing to you?" Molly asked. "When do I get to see him?"

"When I decide to marry him." Jill had recently made a rule that the next person she brought over to Molly would be the one she would marry. "And not before."

When Jill left, Molly turned their conversation over in her mind. There were signals that made her feel panic, some dangerous word Jill had said, or knew about but hadn't said. It was all there, but Molly couldn't piece it together. That night she called Jill.

"When you get ready to introduce me to Dan," said Molly, "I'll have you both to dinner. I'll prepare everything from scratch, and you won't believe how good it is."

"Molly."

"What?"

"All of this is too difficult."

Molly thought she knew what she meant. "I know it," she said. "Come over tomorrow. I'll cut your hair."

William began to stay away from the house more, and as the days went by Molly started to press for some word of affection, but she

did so by asking where he went and accusing him. She tried to think
of new ways to fix her hair. One night William came in late and fell
asleep on the sofa, and Molly thought this was the beginning of the
real end.

"You came in so late," Molly said. "Where were you?"

"Don't start, Molly. I could ask the same about you sometimes."

Some sort of divorce had already occurred—a collapse that had
gone beyond the event of their marriage. The air had changed, and
the arena for love had become as sharp as tin.

"We have to talk," she kept saying to William, but made everything worse with her suggestion. Their moods grew into an activity
of reconnaissance.

Molly went to museums. Sometimes she went with Jill, sometimes alone. She sat before a painting, exploring a line as it went
from one place to another on the canvas. Today she went from room
to room studying how a painter created tall grass with the wind
going through it, or the roundness of a big summer moon, or a root
rubbed smooth and pale as a child's palm.

"Molly?" Someone interrupted her. It was Professor McGinnis
but she called him Ben now. "I called your house. They said you
were here."

Molly assumed he had spoken to Lucas or Franci. She was
shocked that he had followed her here.

"I wanted to talk to you."

She got up to leave, to say she had to go.

"But maybe it's not a good idea."

"Maybe not," she said, though she wanted him to stay.

Ben's class had given her a place to house her hurt mind. She
loved the configurations and the way he described them. The exciting changes, and the reasons for change. The precessional wobble
and the exponential quality of everything. The infinite largeness
she loved. And when Ben McGinnis spoke of these things, his voice
had a storied rhythm, like the murmured consciousness in which a
poem is read, or any dreamlike stance that touches an interior posture.

He pretended to have other business. "I was coming over here anyway. I mean, I was going to the movies."

"Oh."

"Will you be in class?" he asked.

"Yes." She spoke definitely.

He smiled. "Well, I'll see you then."

Neither of them could tell if they had just spoken briefly and without consequence, or if this was one of those times they would look back on and know that at this point, because of Ben's deliberate move, everything had changed.

"We're having a test, a pop test."

"On what?"

"Aberrations of light."

February 24, 1986

Aberration: a deviation from the proper or expected course. (Latin _aberrare_ = to go astray)

Chromatic aberration: The simple refracting telescope brought with it a defect. An image of a star, or edge of a planet, was suffused with a colored halo which destroyed sharpness. So: the _actual_ position and the _apparent_ position of the same star are different. Image of a star is actually a number of images—each a different color and at different distances. Impossible to focus all colors at the same time. The image we see is faulty. This defect is chromatic aberration.

I think about this: how astronomy accepts the fact that what we see is not what is actually there. We make constant corrections. What we see is an aberration and the correction allows us to talk about it. Is this right? Is it right that what is really true must be imagined more than seen?

We are like blind people. All our eyes are white.

On Friday afternoon Molly came home with a car full of groceries, and she called for Joe to help her unload them.

"Did you get Doritos?" He looked until he found the large bag sticking out from the top. He lifted it from the sack.

"Don't eat the whole bag," said Molly. Will sat under the gazebo in the back of the yard, but he started walking toward the house when he saw Molly drive up.

"I'll have supper ready in thirty minutes," she said. They planned to go to a movie. William had called and suggested it. Molly believed he was trying, and she had grown happy in her belief.

"Where're Lucas and Franci?"

"Hunting Mr. Fox."

Whenever Lucas set out to hunt a fox, he called it Mr. Fox, but he was always glad when the trap didn't come down on it. He had made a new trap out of a crate, and Molly looked around the side of the house to see if they had taken it with them. It was gone.

Yesterday Franci described a particular kind of rope they had. "See? It won't break. It's more like wire," and she let her mother test its strength. "We can set it up beside the creek."

"Lucas took bacon for bait," William told her.

"But they never stay this late," Molly said. It was six o'clock. "They know to come home by now."

The last sack of groceries had been put away when Molly looked through the kitchen window and saw Lucas and Franci running toward the house. She thought they had been stung. William saw them at the same time and opened the door.

"What's the matter?" They weren't crying, but their faces looked worse than crying.

"What happened?" Joe put down the Doritos. They had come, not from the woods, but from Caroline's house next door. They had left something at Caroline's.

Lucas didn't have on a shirt and the look of him without his shirt frightened Molly. "Where's your shirt, Lucas?" But Franci spoke first.

She told them slowly about what they had done, but from her expression they knew she wasn't telling it all.

When they reached the tree where they would set up the trap, they wrapped one end of the rope around the lowest limb and arranged the other end so it could lift the fox and catch his neck or legs. They made a sliding knot and put bacon on top of the crate. But whenever they did this before, when the trap door lifted, the rope always came loose and the fox was able to escape. This time, though, was different.

Franci hid behind a bush and held the cord. Lucas usually liked to hold it, but he grew restless and wandered off. Franci didn't see the fox at first, she said, but heard it scrabbling around where the bacon was.

"Lucas! Lucas!" she whisper-yelled. "We caught him! I think we caught him!"

"We did?"

What happened next was what they'd planned, but hadn't imagined actually seeing. The spring set to go off jerked up when Franci pulled the rope. The top opened and closed, and the rope wrapped around the neck of the fox and he was pulled skyward. The little yipe-cry was exaggerated with surprise. Then there was another sound which they thought at first was the crate cracking, but upon close inspection saw it was the neck, or back, of the fox. The rope had not flexed with the rise of the tree limb. It took a little while before the legs stopped jerking and the head rolled around to an odd angle.

But then they saw the worst thing. When the fox swung toward them they could see her milky nipples.

"Did it die?" Lucas couldn't stop looking.

Franci said it did, but she said they had to look around and find its young. "It has some young," she told Lucas. They searched for an hour before they found a hidden covert where the small foxes lay. They had the miserable look of newborns.

"They don't look like foxes," said Lucas. He leaned over to see them. The smell was sour.

Franci said they had to take them home. So Lucas took off his shirt to wrap them in. The mother fox still swung over the crate, and Franci told Lucas to cut it down. He said he couldn't and handed her his knife. Franci did it herself.

They brought the foxes to Caroline's garage and found a basket they had used last year for some baby birds. Franci told all this to her mother, and Lucas didn't speak until she was through. His thin chest, without his shirt, made him seem bony, impatient.

"We left it out there," he finally said. He meant the dead fox. He looked embarrassed to be here.

So William and Molly and Joe followed them back to the place where the fox was, and Joe dug a hole. He suggested they place stones around the grave, Indian-fashion. "So people won't all the time be walking on it," he said. He knew a ritual would help them. Lucas brought a rock much too big to place on the grave, but no one told him it was too big. He still didn't have on a shirt. William offered to carry him home piggyback.

It was three days later when Franci brought the cub foxes into her own garage. Caroline came over to see if she could feed them. Molly was in the kitchen.

"You'll have to ask Franci," Molly said, because last year the baby birds stayed at Caroline's house and Caroline got to decide the times they would be fed. Now Franci wanted the privilege of that decision.

"What'll you do?" Caroline followed Franci to the garage. "I mean, when they get big?"

Franci reached behind the freezer to bring out the basket. It was warm behind the freezer. "I don't know. We'll just do *this* now." The foxes had only the slightest evidence of fox features. They crawled around in the basket like kittens.

"This one's hungry," Franci said and she prepared a stopperful of milk. They watched one suck from the stopper before Franci said, "My daddy didn't come home the other night."

"What do you mean?"

"I mean, he came home, but it was late and I heard Mama yelling at him."

"That doesn't mean anything. Mine fuss all the time."

"Yeah, but does he stay out late?"

"Sometimes." They sounded as if they were bragging. "You should name this one." Caroline held up one ratty fox.

"I already did." Franci took it from her and rubbed its stomach hair with her thumb. Soft red fur was coming in all over him. "This one's Fire."

Caroline touched Fire with a respectful air. "That's a good name."

The crate stayed broken beside the creek. No one brought it home, but Lucas and Franci kept going back to see it. If the water rose, it was carried downstream and they had to search for it again. They always wanted to know just where it was.

Sometimes at the supper table, Lucas said he saw the crate and described it to Molly. But one night Franci told her mother, "Lucas went there by himself today." Her eyes looked foreign. "He said he touched it."

It wasn't until late that Molly bathed and in her nightgown and robe stepped outside to see the stars and the sliver of bright moon. The small foxes slept in the warm basket behind the freezer.

Molly believed more and more in a principle of symmetry operating on a grand scale. She looked for order in the cold stability of bodies rotating, or the wildness of foxes, or pulsars shifting messages. She felt addicted to these connections. After thinking about them, everything else seemed tedious to her.

It was May. William was at home tonight. He stayed upstairs drafting new work. Molly lay down near a bright forsythia bush, but the blossoms were almost gone. The ones left were in the shape of small stars, and their awkward points reminded her not of a real star but of a child's drawing of one.

Earlier in the week Molly had bought new drawing materials and begun work on her *Children in the Sandbox* painting. The season in the painting was winter with a hard, metallic sun. The children wore bright coats, and sand lay spilled around the sides. Two of the children looked like Will. One had his hands, the other had his hair. She tried not to think about it.

A week ago Molly had gone to look through the telescope at Halley's comet. She took Lucas with her that night. Lucas expected to see a long dramatic streak, but what he saw was not even close to being drama.

"What's the big deal?" he said. "I don't see what the big deal is."

William called for Molly to come in, saying that Joe was talking in his sleep. This usually meant he had a fever.

Molly went to Joe's room and felt his forehead. It was twelve-thirty. "You feel okay? You were shouting something."

"I was?" He turned to his mother, still half-asleep. "Do my head?" It was what he asked for as a child when he wanted to think of ways to keep her in his room. Molly moved her fingers across his scalp, letting his hair fall back in silly strands.

He was too old for this, but she was glad to be asked. His hands lay open on the pillow and Molly could see in the vague bathroom light, a small brown mole between his middle and index fingers. She leaned to see it better. Sometimes she felt she didn't know Joe anymore.

"What're you doing?" he stirred, woke up.

"Go back to sleep," she told him.

William was in bed when Molly climbed in beside him, and he turned to curl himself around her back. They slept like spoons, the way they slept all these years. Molly couldn't believe he didn't love her.

The next morning William woke before Molly did. He lay very still in the memory of delirious sweethearted summers, where everything they did—bathing, eating or not eating, the clothes they chose, the cologne they wore—all of it was done for love.

And he turned to Molly, putting his hands into the morning uproar of her hair, and he wanted her. Molly kissed him from her own early memory of how they were. There was an ecstatic tongue in her head as she tasted his neck and face. She kissed his ears and eyes until William dropped his hand onto her pink, babylike breast. She smelled like a warm sauce.

CHAPTER
THREE

What William thought of each time he made love to Molly was how wrong it was. This morning they started with a dreamy desire, but they could see through the filter of the dreaming and weren't able to love each other without the filter, or the dream. So it wasn't that they couldn't love, but rather that neither of them had the courage to love.

Their response was only physical. They knew the difference now. There had been a time when they couldn't distinguish between the physical act and the actual loving. But over the past year William had known what it was to perform, and he knew even in the pleasure of the performance that what he had felt for Molly was gone.

He couldn't remember not loving Molly. Even at nineteen, it seemed he had loved her all his life, so months ago when he said he didn't love her, it felt like a lie.

God knows, William thought, I feel old and small.

He could hear Lucas watching the Saturday morning cartoons. For the past four years William had watched these with him. They got up at six o'clock, and even though William might doze through most of the programs, he could hear Lucas say, "Watch this, Dad. This is the *best* one," about each new cartoon that came on.

Lucas was lying on the sofa when William walked into the den. "Scoot over," he told him.

"You gonna watch these with me?"

It was a new show about robots fighting wars for people. "This is the best one, Dad. Watch this."

During the next commercial William asked, "Have you had breakfast?" and offered to fix the breakfast they ate when Lucas was four and five—grilled cheese sandwiches. Lucas yelled approval at the suggestion of grilled cheeses, and William felt, as he sometimes did, the fun of his life coming back. He didn't know how to keep it, though. He felt it come back, then slip away again.

"Why are you so unhappy?" Molly had asked him. She had never been unhappy in the way William was now. Not in his way.

"I don't want to talk about it. I can't talk about things and feel better the way you do, Molly."

"Maybe we should get some help."

"That's the last thing we should get." Every time they tried to talk, William felt as though he had climbed into a crawl space under the house.

"What *else* is on?" Franci came in. She no longer watched cartoons, or claimed not to, but she joined them and ate the crusts of bread they tore off and left on their plates. "I never watch this stuff."

"*We're* watching this." Lucas was afraid Franci might horn in on them.

"But you've been watching what you want all morning. I get to pick *one* thing."

"What do you want to watch, honey?" William asked her.

"What's on?"

"*See?* She doesn't even know what's *on*. I'm not changing it." Lucas poured himself a glass of juice. Franci went to the kitchen to get some food for herself, and William tried to talk Lucas into changing the channel. Lucas' protest came out teary.

"That's okay," Franci yelled. "I don't want to watch it anyway." Neither of them knew why she gave in so easily.

Molly was up. They could hear her in the shower.

Sometimes Saturdays got long and William tried to think of what they could do. Molly stuck her head around the door and asked whether anyone would mind if she worked on some paintings today. Her hair dripped from its pile of bobby pins, and she had on only a few clothes.

On the afternoon of their marriage, Molly had stepped into the chapel with her hair piled on her head and lace coming off her like water. Some of her hair was gathered around her forehead and neck, deliberately pulled out, not to look deliberate. Her eyes had a directness that indicated she was devoted to her instincts, and the veil that came down over her head and face did not cover her full mouth. William had known her for three years before they married, but he had never seen her like this, her mouth. He didn't worry about happiness then. He didn't know when he lost it.

It occurred to William to ask Molly if she would watch cartoons with them, but she had never done this, so he didn't know how to include her now. If they hadn't made love this morning, Molly might have said something petulant or resistant, but their performance changed the tone of the day so that their anger would go in different directions now. No one wanted to say how bad it was.

He was glad for her to work in her studio, and told her so. The sun came pouring in from the porch, and nests of flower baskets bloomed on the steps. He said he might wait for Joe to get up and they could go fishing. It was a good idea, Molly told him. So the day shifted, and William felt again his memory of being happy.

The yard was fresh-cut and the windows of the house all open. It was full spring, and the warm air muffled the hard beatings of their pulse and made a pocket for the friendship they retained.

"Come on, Dad. 'Teenage Mutant Ninja Turtles' is on."

"What is _that?_"

"It's _great!_"

"_The eagle when it is old flies so high that it scorches its feathers,_" said Franci.

"Where do you _get_ that stuff?" William laughed.

"But it gets young again by falling into shallow water."

"I'm not believing that!" said Lucas. He pulled his dad in to watch huge turtles speaking with accents.

During the fall of Joe's sophomore year, he began to read about the history of Indians. He couldn't get enough of it, especially when he discovered Chief Joseph of the Nez Percé. Then he loved the Sioux, subjecting himself to uninteresting texts just to get more information about that tribe. He read the Cherokee language. Those sounds moved into his head like water and streaked his mind.

Joe spent his junior year in American history working on a paper about Chief Joseph: "The Time He Thought There Was Peace." In math class he designed a project that put together a portion of land and how it changed hands over a period of a hundred years. He titled it "Diminishing Returns." For the art department he painted a map indicating the routes particular tribes took toward Canada.

It all seemed clear to him—one story that said something about how greed can blossom. He was obsessed and always had something to say about it. Franci and Lucas went crazy with the boredom of all his facts, but William encouraged Joe's soapbox stance and told Molly how good it was to get worked up over these matters.

"It's getting him ready," William said.

For years William had studied the period of history around World War II the same way, and Molly thought herself deprived and stupid that she had never felt passionate about any period of history. She wanted to be one of those people who found a subject to pursue, then discover a sweet secret about themselves, finally seeing through the filter of what was learned. To take knowledge—facts, stories, equations, whatever it was—and learn to breathe under the water of that place. People who did this found out how alive they were.

When Joe came downstairs, it was past noon. Lucas had gone to play with Johnny, and Franci was at the mall with Caroline. William pointed to the two lunches in paper sacks he had prepared and suggested Joe go fishing with him. He had worms in a jar, and fishing poles stood propped on the back steps.

Joe acted glad, but his expression said he didn't care much about going. It used to be the other way around, with Joe asking his dad to go somewhere and his dad not wanting to, but going anyway.

"Listen, I have to be back at four," Joe said. He was two inches taller than his father. He added a full bag of Doritos and stuck two apples into his sack. "It's been a couple of years since we've done this." Joe spoke with pleasure, but William heard it in guilt.

"What happens at four?" William asked.

"We play poker at Andrew's house. We have a running game on Saturday nights."

"Who taught you poker?"

"Mom did."

They walked to a place that didn't look familiar to William, but Joe said, "The last time we were here, I caught a trout. Remember? Right over there." Joe pointed downstream. William didn't remember the place at all.

"I remember," he said, and reached into the bag to pull out their sandwiches. Joe propped his pole and kept it steady between his knees while he ate. William sat beside him.

"What's the matter with you and Mom?" Joe asked this so quickly that William couldn't swallow and had to chew a long time before answering.

It was not the way he wanted to bring it up. He wanted to have a different mood when they talked about it. Joe wore a sweatshirt and William's favorite socks. His hair had not been combed, and the look he gave his father was so unwavering that William felt the pressure to explain everything with the clarity of a professional.

"What makes you ask that?" he said. "We're just having some trouble." He tried to speak honestly.

Joe heard it as honest. "Mom says you're not happy." Their faces plumbed each other's as though each thought the other might be deaf.

William knew that when it all came apart, people would ask the reason he and Molly had split up, and they might think it was because he'd fallen in love with someone, or maybe it was something Molly had done. Molly might even say those things herself. So William would need to think of a reason—the truth being that he didn't know what had happened to them. He could see sometimes where it all ended, but not where it started to end. Though if anyone asked, he would have an answer and might give different answers at different times. He pictured himself doing so.

"She told you that?" William wondered when they had talked about it.

"I asked her and she said it. It's true, isn't it?"

He guessed it was. This was not the way he wanted to talk. "Listen, Joe," William said, but Joe interrupted him.

"A lot of my friends' parents have split." And Joe told his father with that one statement that he knew it might happen and even if it did, he had already forgiven it. But Joe had no way of knowing how much there was to forgive.

"What do you mean?" William couldn't believe what Joe said.

"I mean," Joe sounded more like the father giving advice to the son, "it happens. I know people who've gone through it."

William needed to say something, but at that moment Joe got a bite on his line and they moved their attention to fishing. They didn't get back to the subject.

At three-thirty Joe pulled out his line. "I have to go," he said. "You stay." He thought his dad was having fun. "Why don't you stay?"

"Fine. Tell your mother you caught a fish and I'll bring it when I come."

Joe stood up. "Listen, Dad, this was fun."

"It was great," William told him. He waited until Joe was all the way across the clearing and out of sight before he wrapped his pole and decided to walk in a direction away from the creek.

Two men, George Kirby and another man, were on their way to the creek with their young sons. The boys looked excited with what they were about to do, and the fathers talked. William wanted to tell them how soon the boys wouldn't care about coming here. He wanted to warn them not to be so happy.

William's father died before he could know him well. William claimed that most fathers died before their sons could know them. He was ten that year and it was the same year he had begun the job of cleaning the well.

He had a newspaper route and did odd jobs around the house to earn money. He had been introduced to sex in magazines by this age and was flashing fantasies at night. He had never talked to his father about these things and fretted now over who should be his confessor. There was an older brother. He was the one who had shown Will the magazine sex, but Will couldn't confide easily in Ted. Ted was five years older and wasn't home most of the time. He hoped his mother wouldn't expect Ted to try to take his father's place. He hoped he wouldn't be expected to do so either.

William's father had gotten up one morning as usual, showered, and put on one sock before he fell. He died instantly, the doctors said. He was naked except for that sock, and young William found him. He went to the bathroom to ask his father to take him to school. But Edward Hanner lay slumped in a peculiar fashion on the bathroom floor, his arm still on the tub. The death of his father and the job of cleaning the well were linked in William's mind.

Always in the spring and sometimes in the early fall, William's mother said, "Time to clean the well," and William shuddered, or a shudder went through him. He put on jeans he saved for well-cleaning and a shirt he didn't care about. He got a rope and the plank to sit on. His mother made a mixture for cleaning, one that was strong but not poisonous.

Tess Hanner lowered William into the well and held him with the strength of a man. When she rigged a row of double rope, William trusted how sure it would be.

She used what was called inch rope—an inch thick. If the rope looked at all frayed, Tess sent to Ralph Hancock's store to get a new one. She tied knots and rechecked each one. Her hands worked in quick movements, as if she were using thread instead of rope. She wrapped it around a big black winch to roll and unroll it. It was hard not to believe in that rope's thickness.

Before she lowered William into the well, she tied another rope around his waist and one to a tree. She loosened it as he went down. He started out, not at the top, but not too far down—about half-way—so that at first there was plenty of light still coming in where he was. He could see the tops of trees and the blue sky. He could see the clouds moving fast, and the outline of his mother's hair as she leaned into the well to call him.

"Will? You all right?" William yelled back that he was fine. "Call to me every now and then, so I'll know."

"I'm okay." He could see her head and shoulders as she leaned. "You're going to fall in," he told her.

"Not until I'm ready."

He knew she smiled, even though her face was directed away from the light. All the light lay behind her, and her head and shoulders and hair had a simple outline. And even though he couldn't see the features on her face (her face completely dark), he knew she smiled because of the different way words sound when the mouth is smiling and when it's not. Then she moved over and the sunlight she had blocked came back in. The experience was similar to the passing of an eclipse.

The scrubbing ritual took two days.

After he scrubbed the wall with the sun on it, he scrubbed the dark side and had to use a flashlight, so the task demanded more concentrated attention. Sometimes he forgot about his mother until she called down to him again. When he answered from so deep, his voice sounded altered.

William was afraid at that depth. He was afraid of the wet, dark wall and the cold, pungent mineral smell that had the odor of blood, and of the air—thick and kind of oily.

He didn't know what his mother did during the time he scrubbed. He knew she brought a ladder-back chair to sit in. When he shouted for her to lower him more, she did so as gently and slowly as she could. Finally he could no longer see the tops of trees or even a small piece of sky.

One time when she pulled him up, it was a bright day and they had lunch. But as she started to let him down again, he said he didn't want to do it. He told her he was afraid.

"That's the fear of your own death," she told him. But William didn't think that was it. He was young and didn't think much about his own death. Tess said she used to go into caves with her uncles. She hated it, she said, but she went. And she always thought as she entered the mouth that she might die there. So after lunch, when William was lowered again, he was more afraid than if he hadn't said anything.

Sometimes while he was in the well he could hear his mother singing. She sang songs he had never heard on the radio or in church, though her voice, as she sang, sounded a little bit like church. As the day went on she sang louder, and William didn't know if she did so because he was further down, or because the day was ending. He finally decided that these were songs she made up herself, and that this was probably the only time she sang them.

"When I was yo-ung I fell in love / and a-al-l the world grew free. / When I got older Love came do-wn / and to-ok the heart o-of me."

"Who broke your heart?" William asked his mother one day in the kitchen. He was nineteen and had already met Molly.

His mother shook her head. "Many times," she told him. Then she said, "You will."

"I never will," he promised, but he could see her smile, not a real one, not one meant to be a smile. This time her features were not blackened by shadows, but clear. The light of a lamp was behind her, and sun came through the windows and trees and made her look like a speckled bird.

William knew now that he did break her heart, and his own, and others. He didn't know how much it had to do with his memory of the high red wall and oily air or his mother's inch-rope.

Last Tuesday night William had seen Carol for a few minutes before going home. When she met him at the door, her face brightened to see him and he told her he was leaving Molly soon. But even though he said it, he couldn't picture himself doing it. There were always reasons not to leave. He sat down at Carol's table and took her hand. He wanted to pretend that she meant everything in the world to him.

William couldn't think of his life without Joe or Franci or Lucas. And at the times when he tried to think of it, he grew very still, so that nothing in his life seemed true. Sometimes in that stillness he thought he could smell something burning, a burnt smell. Why was that? When someone is afraid of doing something radically different, did it burn like that? Did it leave an actual ash somewhere in the brain, or heart? William thought it probably did.

The ground was muddy with spring, and it collapsed slightly with each step he took. William had walked for fifteen minutes past the woods and when he looked up he was standing in a field of goats. The air was cool, and he felt punished by the surprise of where he was.

Molly was not at home when William got back, so he went to his favorite spot at the far end of the yard near the gazebo. When she drove up, she waved and asked what he wanted for dinner. She gave him a choice between chicken and steak.

He said chicken if she would make that mustard sauce.

"And rice?"

To hear them talking from a distance, if a neighbor heard, the tone would be defined as pleasant, more than pleasant. When they moved into that mode, they believed it was true. Molly brought a drink out to William.

"Where's the fish Joe caught?" she asked.

William had left it at the stream. His expression said he had.

"Well, something's made a good meal of it by now."

Franci and Lucas came around the side of the house, running. They had been to the garage to feed the foxes, but one had died and Franci looked prematurely grief-stricken about losing another one.

"If they don't drink from this stopper, they'll *all* die." Lucas stood beside her and held the offending fox. He stood quiet in the wake of Franci's words.

Molly took the fox and the stopper of milk. "You have to touch him," she said. She stroked his head and neck with her thumb. "Here, and here." So Franci touched him and so did Lucas, until finally the fox began to suck.

After dinner they sat on the porch. Usually they watched TV, but neither wanted to tonight. William read the paper and Molly sketched the yard. The moon was low and orange through the trees, big with lunacy. She thought of the constellations she would see tonight and checked the sky like it was a room to be put on display.

"Did you know that in a binary star system," Molly told them at supper, "one of the stars might be invisible?" She leaned forward to get the attention of everyone. "And the only way you know it's there is by the path of the companion star—the way it circles around and around the invisible one." She compared this to relationships. "It's like saying, 'I didn't know you were married,' or maybe 'Was that your brother?'"

Molly had tacked sketches on the kitchen wall showing which constellations sat high during a particular month. And lately when she talked about these things, her voice grew pleasing, so that she had to remind herself that these were "merely stars."

March 9, 1986

Who knows but what these systems are not projections of our own systems? What if the stars and their companions are subject to the same rules we understand for ourselves? What if the manipulation and balance of each other are already determined by the galaxy we live in?

Sometimes she told the family about the discovery of a comet or a star in a distant galaxy. The star or comet would be named after the person who found it, or else that person could name it. When she told them these things, Lucas asked, "Is this going to take *long*?" But Joe listened. "Shhh," he told Lucas. "Let her tell it." Joe's interest in Indians had dropped off, but he understood obsession when he saw it.

William did not speak at dinner and was openly quiet as he sat on the porch. He hadn't spoken about anything of consequence for days, though he admitted to Molly and to himself that he couldn't find a track for his work.

He used to learn through images, the way Molly did. They had that in common. His first architectural project was based on an image of his mother's dress. On the dress were three peacocks, and the memory of them had loosened his mind.

The wings of the peacocks lay completely open. One fan opening onto the front of her skirt covered her entire lap. One lay across her shoulder, and though the other shoulder was not bare, it seemed bare because of the absence of color. The last peacock spread across the back, low, with the head sticking up beneath the belt. Its fan filled the seat of her skirt and was partly hidden as it turned under for the generous hem.

Tess Hanner bragged about this dress and its four-inch hem. But even if this had not been her favorite dress, it would be the one William liked the most. He liked the way her body moved in it, and the inclination of her breasts and hips when she leaned or walked. None of her other dresses were like this one. When she wore it, her arms flew around her, liberating expressions of mischief.

It was the arrangement of the peacocks that opened William to new ideas. His assignment was to draw a plan for a museum to be situated in the outskirts of a big city. He designed the structure by imagining the settling of birds on a woman's body. The power of the peacocks and the freedom of one shoulder gave him the symmetry he needed. The project won a prize.

The result was a structure which stood both historic and reso-
nant. The inside of the museum had the mysterious quality of that
deep-length hem, and could give to even the most banal person a
taste for the arts.

William continued to use the peacock image, but it grew stale.
Then, several years later, he designed an office building for a suburb
in Asheville, and for a while he brought back his rag of intention.
Every time he rode by the building, he thought how he must be on
some new track, but the confidence didn't stay. Something, he didn't
know what, was trying to break the male in him. He couldn't say
how this was happening.

"Miz Hanner? Is Joe here?" Andrew Hawkins ran up the porch
steps. He only nodded a greeting to William, because William
looked so distracted. "Is he upstairs?" He thought no one had heard
him. Andrew was tall, a skinny, dark-haired boy with simian arms
and the face of a young Clint Eastwood.

"He was going to your house," Molly said. "He was about to
leave."

Andrew nodded another greeting to William, then went to see if
Molly had any cookies or brownies. He knew where to look and
would take one, if any were there.

"I go to my class tonight," Molly said. It was not yet dark, though
almost seven o'clock.

"Tonight?" William could never remember when she had her
class.

"I left some brownies in the cake tin. They're probably still
warm."

"Okay, thanks." His answer seemed in accordance with some instruction. He wished he could sound different. "I don't know if I'll
still be up."

But when Molly got in from class that night, William had waited
for her, and they made popcorn and poured beer into huge mugs.
William suggested they watch a rerun of "Gunsmoke."

In the middle of the barroom fight, William touched Molly and a light, dry roiling curled in the bright globe of her head. He reached around to feel the rim of her spine and the soft play of her neck. "Molly." He loved her and thought for a moment that it had all come back and that everything else had been a terrible misunderstanding.

But when he entered her and Molly screamed slightly, he felt again the lack of courage and thought how he did not love her anymore. He was afraid he might not ever be able to love anyone again. And it was as though he had shouted it out roughly into her ear. She heard how he no longer loved her, even though William had not stopped his fine circular motion above her, and she had not finished rolling and pressing beneath him. They tried hard to make up for the invisible shout.

And when William came inside her, he felt himself spread flat and hot. In a few moments Molly stopped her own slow moving and as they both pulled away, Molly said, "That's all, Will."

And William knew he had been let go.

CHAPTER
FOUR

William did not leave the next day. But a few weeks later, in the middle of May, he came home for supper. It was a Wednesday night and he was earlier than usual. Molly stood in the kitchen preparing his favorite fettuccine dish.

"We'll eat in a little while." She pointed to a large platter of noodles, steaming. "You're early." She said it like an accusation.

"Nobody's here?"

"No." She stirred some sauce onto the noodles to let him taste. He couldn't do it.

"Molly." He said her name so plainly and in such a straight manner that Molly couldn't mistake it for anything but what it was.

"You are leaving," she told him as plainly as he had said her name.

He took a spoonful of the fettuccine and held it in his mouth a moment before swallowing. She almost asked him to sit down first, to eat before he left for good. She stirred the noodles to even out the place where he had tasted.

He went to the hall closet and she heard him drag out a suitcase. She couldn't hear the drawers in their bedroom open and close and knew he was getting things as quietly as he could. In what seemed only a few moments, William came downstairs and Molly saw he had chosen their oldest, most battered luggage to take with him. She finished adding sauce to the noodles and took rolls out of the oven. The whole house smelled like bread.

"You want to take some of this with you?" Molly offered him a plate. Neither of them mentioned how permanent this might be. They had been married so long that the permanence of the marriage was more real than the permanence of this leaving. "You could take it on a paper plate," she said.

William laughed a little, then he took one long, awkward step toward her. She put her arms around his neck. The wooden spoon she had used to stir the sauce dripped onto William's shirt. "If you do this," she said, "I'm not sure we can ever put it back." She wanted him to know what could be broken.

During the moments before William answered, his mind answered a thousand times, and though he didn't say anything, he made a sound in his throat and that sound was a definite statement about his decision to go. Upon leaving he forgot to pick up the jacket he'd laid on the back of the kitchen chair. Molly didn't remind him to take it.

She added more butter to the noodles and could hear him going down the driveway. She heard him pause just before pulling out into the street. He paused longer than it took to look both ways, and Molly didn't know, honestly, at that moment, if he had come back in, if already it would be too late. She thought how quickly, within moments, a thing can be so completely broken.

"Did Dad leave?" Lucas came in and spoke before Molly saw him. She caught her breath.

"Oh, Lucas, you scared me. Don't do that."

"Was that Dad?" He had seen his dad pull out, and Molly wondered how he would remember this moment when he knew.

"Yes." Had William seen Lucas? "Did he see *you*?"

"I don't think so. He didn't wave." Lucas scooted into the seat where his dad's jacket was. "I want him to help me with history."

"I'll help."

"You can't explain it good."

"Joe can help you."

"I want Dad. When'll he be home?"

Molly put a large helping of fettuccine onto Lucas' plate and asked where Franci was. She handed him a roll. "Don't start yet."

Franci came in the front door and threw her books down. When she saw Lucas she told him he was in her chair.

"So what?"

"Is this all we have?" Franci didn't like fettuccine.

"Yes." Molly opened the refrigerator and took out a dish. "But there's some leftover chicken, if you want it cold."

Franci filled her plate with a small portion of noodles and some chicken. She told her mother it did look good though. Franci was always able to recognize if something seemed wrong.

"Where's Joe?" Franci asked. As she asked, Joe's car drove up and Molly thought when she heard it that it might be William. She believed that this was all a foolish mistake, or else that maybe she was being fooled.

Joe came in sweaty from baseball practice. He had on cleats and said he was hungry. Molly didn't tell him to remove his cleats, nor did she remind them to wash their hands. They thought she'd forgotten. She placed the platter of fettuccine in the middle of the table and put the cold chicken out, and rolls. Her clothes felt shapeless on her skin, like garments in a closet. She tried to think of a way to tell them about this, because William hadn't thought about how he had forced that task on her.

She could take a walk after supper, to think of what to say. Daylight saving time had begun, and even though it was six o'clock, the sun looked like afternoon. "I love it like this," Franci said, and no one knew if she meant the afternoon look or the noodles. She ate the fettuccine as well as the leftover chicken. She wanted to cheer up her mother.

Lucas asked who could help with his history report. Joe claimed to have a lot of homework and said he had to use the phone.

"Before anybody does anything," Molly said, sounding like her old self, "you have to clear these dishes. I'm going for a walk." Her request was not unusual. She did this on many nights during the summer months.

"But who's going to help *me*?" Lucas lamented.

Molly went along the road into town. She walked for almost a mile before looking up, and when she did she saw she was only a couple of blocks from the drugstore. She hoped she would speak in a normal way if she saw someone she knew. Her body felt a capacity for echo and space, and she was afraid that if she spoke the sound coming out might be more like that of a wild goose, or an owl. She wanted to do something that would repudiate the distance she felt between her own heart muscles and the downward chink in her mind. She spoke to a dog and waved to two people on a porch.

She planned a long, elaborate speech to say when she got home, but as she went over the speech, she shortened the long version, and by the time she reached the drugstore and the dog, she had settled on something palatable, maybe even hopeful, to say.

She didn't know if what she felt now was sadness or an absorbed amazement. Her hair was held with a large clip at the back of her neck, and each step she took had a false assertion. Some inexpert puppeteer jounced her arms and legs to make her posture appear twitched and interrupted. If anyone had seen her open the door of the drugstore, it would look as if she expected to be hit by a gush of dark water. The dog had followed her and when Molly saw him she said, "Go home now." Her rhetoric also came from the incapable puppeteer. The dog lay down and waited for Molly to come back out.

Molly didn't see anyone she knew. She bought a new lipstick and some rouge powder she had never bought before. "I just thought I would try it," she explained to the cosmetics lady, as though she needed an excuse for buying something at this particular time. She went home carrying a small sack, because she also bought Hershey Bars for Franci and Joe and Sweet Tarts for Lucas. She would help Lucas with his report before telling them anything. As she walked, it seemed as though she could see tiny contracted points of light advance toward her. She decided to go back by a different route.

Before Molly went into the house, she opened the door to the storage room off the garage and tried to lift a box she had been looking for to store old shoes. The box was filled with William's sports equipment.

"Damn," she muttered. Joe heard her and came out from the kitchen.

"What's the matter?"

"This box. I can't lift it."

"It's got Dad's stuff in it. Leave it. What do you need it for?"

"I need it for my shoes." She sounded desperate, even to herself.

"What's the matter?" Joe didn't know what to think. "Leave it. Dad'll move it when he gets home. What's the matter?"

"He's not coming home." It came out just like that. No speech. No hopeful tone. She wanted to take it back, or alter it and make this seem like something else, but she said it again, softer. Joe stood for long seconds before his face contorted into an expression Molly had seen in him as a boy, but hadn't seen in a long time.

He hid his contortion and spoke into his hands. "I can't believe it," he said. He was so tall, even when he leaned over. But Molly could see how he did believe it, how he needed no more explanation.

"I didn't mean to tell you like this," she said, but she couldn't think now of the way she did mean to say it.

Franci and Lucas had cleaned the kitchen and expected to be praised for the job. They waited for Molly to notice.

"I have something to say," said Molly. Joe stood behind her, trying to look older. He did look older. He looked forty or sixty, the way he stood behind her.

She told them their father had gone away for a while, and the way she said it did not sound permanent.

"Where?" Lucas wanted to know.

They went into the den, moving as though they were guests. They sat on the sofa and in chairs, not on the floor as they usually did. No one at that moment sat on the floor.

"Will he come back?" Franci indicated that she believed he would. She pulled at her sweater, trying to think about it.

"I know what," Lucas said. The way he understood it, his father might be lost or something, so Lucas suggested they go look for him. He thought William might be wandering in some pitiful way along a back road—like the time they lost Buster and found him on a road that went toward Asheville. Lucas was three when Buster went off and he thought he would never see him again, but then they did find him and for months tried to guess what made him wander off. They suspected someone had taken him away.

"I'm going to look for him." Joe spoke suddenly, and Lucas looked pleased that someone wanted to follow his suggestion.

"Oh, honey, you can't do that." Molly strove to see beyond her own confusion. She opened the small sack and gave them the candy. They took it without comment and went to the car.

After forty-five minutes they returned, but no one said where they had been. Molly didn't ask. She told them it was time for bed, wanting them to feel that their schedule was normal, and she tucked everyone in, even Joe.

"I looked everywhere I could think." Joe thought he had failed. He hoped to find his dad and even pictured bringing him back. Joe thought he could make his father do anything.

Lucas said nothing. But when Molly sat on the edge of his bed, he told her there was an Indian Guide meeting for fathers and sons and he didn't know what he would do now. He talked as though his father had died.

"Well, I'm sure he'll go with you, Lucas. All you have to do is ask him about it. He loves that kind of thing." Molly smiled and Lucas turned over. He didn't want to look at her.

They slept that night as separate as cells. The long night and the ritual of sleep kept them separate. Molly tried to think of what was going on in their minds, if it was the same or different from what was going on in her own mind. She tried to imagine the mind of the house, imagining the house had a mind right now, and if you could see it it might look like the coals of a fire gone down—fiery, but without much warmth.

It was five past three when Franci climbed into bed with Molly. Molly was not asleep.

"Is it for *good*?" Franci asked.

"What?" It seemed a strange question to apply to this.

"Did he leave for *good*?"

"I think so." Saying it made everything too large. "But you'll see him a lot. It probably won't be all that different." Molly didn't know why she said this, but Franci believed it. She pulled back the covers and they curled up together as though it were a cold night.

"Will we still live here? I mean, in this house?" Franci asked the next day. One of her close friends moved away when the parents divorced. "Will we have to move?"

Franci was on the brink of losing her tomboyishness. Over the last year she had begun to develop breasts and a definite curviness to her waist.

"You can't wear my shirts anymore," Joe told her last week when he got tired of seeing all his favorite T-shirts on her floor. "You leave tit-marks on them!"

"Tit-marks!" Lucas rolled over laughing, embarrassed for Franci.

"Come here." Joe took Lucas up to his room for who-knows-what kind of lesson. They closed the door.

Molly could picture the kind of woman Franci would be. She loved this daughter as she did no one else in the world. She thought of her own mother and opened the window to let in the drowsy precipitation of spring.

"We won't move, Franci," Molly promised, but she didn't know if it was a promise she would keep.

It was three days before she told Jill. She asked the children not to mention it either, but she felt sure there were rumors and wondered, as she dialed Jill's number, if Jill already knew.

"I want to come over for a while," Molly said. She didn't say why she wanted to come.

"Come right now," Jill said. It took ten minutes for Molly to get to Jill's front door.

"Will's moved out." Molly spoke before she had crossed the living room to sit down. "He's moved into an apartment on Cedar Street." The windows behind Jill were tall and Molly couldn't tell yet what her expression was.

"When?"

"Wednesday."

"You should've called me, Molly." There was a silence as though Molly had spoken of death. "What about the kids?"

"Joe expected it to happen, but I don't think he expected to be as shocked as he was. He's so sad. Franci thinks it's her fault somehow. She asked if it was something she had done. And Lucas—I don't know what Lucas's thinking."

"You think he'll want to come back?" Jill didn't want to imply that he should.

"I don't think so." But the truth of the matter was that Molly did think he would come back and that maybe next week or month their life could be restored to order. She didn't know what else to think.

"I shouldn't be surprised," said Jill, "but I am."

"You know, Jill, I think Will probably stayed with me until my mother died. I mean, until all that sickness part was over. I think he didn't want me to be alone when that happened."

"You're probably right." And though they talked another two hours, Molly found this remark to be the most comforting; it felt so good to be right about one thing.

During the day Lucas pretended nothing had happened, but at night he called out with bad dreams, or woke up scared and said it was a dream. How could she have prepared him for this?

"It happens all the time," people told her, as though this could make her feel better. But those who said it did not think it would happen to them.

As the weeks went on and it became clear that William would not come home, Lucas grew clingy. He resented any time his mother spent alone. He even knocked incessantly on the bathroom door if her bathroom time grew to be too long.

"I have to get in there."

"Go to the other bathroom, honey."

"I can't."

"Why not?"

"Franci's in there."

"I'll be out in a minute, Lucas."

"I *have* to." She could tell he leaned his head against the bathroom door, that he had his forehead against it. His hand turned the knob back and forth. "*Now!*"

So Molly pulled out of the warm water, wrapped a towel around her, checked the clock to see that her bathroom time had not exceeded six minutes but was two minutes longer than last night, and opened the door for Lucas.

"You getting out?" He spoke as though he had inadvertently interrupted her.

"Yes."

"What're you gonna do now?" He forgot to lift the lid.

"Lucas! Put the lid up first!" He lifted it, but urine splashed on the floor. "Lucas!"

"Sorry." He zipped himself and wiped the floor.

"I think I'll work on some sketches," she said in answer to his question. She dried her legs and thought nothing of standing naked before him. The steamy bathroom had made her hair a mass of tangled curls.

"'Family Ties' is on!"

"No," she said and covered herself again.

"Mama!" Franci yelled from downstairs. "'Family Ties' is on." They watched it together.

"Where's Joe?" Molly asked when it was over.

"He's staying at Dad's."

"You know what?" Molly told Lucas. "You're almost as tall as Franci."

Lucas walked in front of his mother. He took her to the place at the stream where he caught crayfish. He thought she wanted to see them.

"A whole pool of them," he bragged. He brought a bucket and would take a few home.

"What do you do with them?" But Lucas avoided the question, because sometimes he forgot and let them die in a bucket or in the carport.

"We put them in the sewer pipe," he said, because once he left them there, and they lived.

Molly put her hand on his head. "You'll be taller than I am before you know it." Lucas expanded with pleasure at the expression of his height. He led the way downstream, farther than Molly had been before. In a while they came to a waterfall. The water was nearly thirty feet high, and because of recent rains its force was heavy. Lucas told her it hardly ever got this big.

"But sometimes it does," he said, and pointed to a place behind the falls where they could stand. He had been there before and took off his shirt and shoes to crawl over the rocks and get behind the water. Before Molly knew what he was doing, Lucas stood in the shallow pool. It came up to his knees and he called for his mother to join him. He said he was not even getting wet.

Molly laid her shoes behind the pile of Lucas' clothes, rolled up her jeans, and climbed over the rocks to where he was. "Is this where the crayfish are?" she asked before stepping in.

"No." He pointed to a separate pool to the left of the waterfall.

The water poured in front of them and Molly couldn't describe, even to herself, what it was like to stand behind it. Part of it was the water, part of it was that Lucas brought her here. The noise kept them from hearing each other, but she could hear pieces of what Lucas said, and she felt the privilege of his inclusion.

All around them was green—the low-hanging trees on either side and even the rocks behind them were covered with lichen. But the best part and what Lucas wished to show her was the way you could see through the falls—the distortion of trees and the whole view of blue-grey-green blurring in a way that made the colors seem everything and the shapes nothing.

Neither of them saw at first the man at the edge of the stream.

Neither of them saw his hard, wide face and his left hand held slightly behind his leg. Lucas saw him and touched his mother's arm, and Molly felt the center of herself grow cold.

They climbed back over the rocks, soaking wet and noticed that the man had moved their pile of clothes to a place farther from the stream. Molly felt alarm when she saw that he had moved their clothes.

The man's gaze toward them did not change. So she told Lucas to put on his shoes and shirt, but she said it in a natural voice. Her hands helped to hurry him. As she worked to get Lucas dressed, Molly spoke cheerfully to the man. She pretended his face had a regular expression, or else that maybe it would have, if she spoke to him this way.

"I've never been here before," she told him, though he hadn't spoken to her yet. He seemed about to speak. "My son and I were just walking." She knew she sounded formal and that she must look frightened. She didn't know how to keep from it.

She stooped down to pretend to do something to Lucas' shoe and whispered, "Run. Get some help," but as she said it she heard the man speak.

"Just a minute."

She pushed Lucas away. "Yes?" she said, as though they were in a department store and he had asked to make a purchase. Lucas ran into the woods, toward their house, but Molly ignored his running. When the man turned to see him, she said, "He'll be right back."

The man stood slightly closer now, so that Lucas was behind him, far behind, running, and so was Molly's whole mind. She could see a brown mark on his cheek and she stared very intently at that spot, because it made him seem like any ordinary person.

He scruffed the toe of his boot into the ground beside them. He looked like a hairy farmer as he squinted sideways, and with a sluggish stir, he studied Molly's hot face. Molly had no thoughts while he was doing this. Her mind lay in front of her blank as a page.

"I have to go now," she announced in answer to his "Just a minute." Each word they said sounded practiced.

The man twitched when she spoke and when he moved she could see in his left hand, slightly behind his leg, a glint of metal on a knife. When she saw it, a thunder rolled into her and made everything around them seem precious and soft. Then he walked toward her saying something, though she couldn't tell exactly what he said. He mumbled something about a fire, where he had built a fire.

And for a moment as he came toward her, she thought of getting into a lower position, of scrunching down into a squat the way animals take a subordinate place in recognition of power, and how sometimes it prevents a fight. She thought of sitting on the ground but couldn't make her legs move or bend.

When he stood two feet from her, he seemed not a person but a square structure, and she felt absorbed into his empty, smoke-colored hair. She thought she could pace around inside him like he was a room. He seemed as empty as that. His gaze seemed that bare.

And he pointed to a place beside her foot where a fire had been, so Molly realized that he camped here. Maybe it was where he lived. He had a sore on his leg that needed tending. His pants were torn and she could see the gash near his knee. It was open and he limped slightly with the infection of it.

If she ran—she was afraid he might chase her. She didn't think she could outrun him. She didn't even know if she could step to the side a few inches, but she did move. She stepped sideways away from the place that he said was his fire, and said yes, she could see it, but she didn't say that there had not been a fire there in a while, and she didn't know exactly what he was seeing, his eyes so secret with drama.

"I'll go now," she said.

She hadn't noticed the noise of the waterfall for a few minutes but noticed it now and the difference between how she felt now (with him close) and how she felt before (when he wasn't here) was like the difference between aluminum and wood.

"No," he said and took hold of her arm. He did this so fast that

Molly shivered, and though she found words, part of her voice had been subtracted and she spoke in short breaths.

He asked her to stay, and his voice was nice, polite almost, as he put down his knife. He said he had seen them behind the waterfall and that he wanted to get behind it too. He said he lived in a small shack and pointed deeper in the woods. Molly thought of him left out here like a neglected child.

He took off his shirt. He said for her to climb with him behind the falls, and Molly thought of a thousand things: of running, of picking up the knife. She thought of being overpowered, and of Lucas and where he was. The man motioned for her to climb over the rocks. And though he didn't seem as harmful as he had moments before, she wasn't sure of anything until they both stood knee-deep in the small pool with water like a wide sheet in front of them.

"Sometimes I come here," he said. When he spoke his gaze focused on the water, a blurred, no-shape veil, and he spoke into it. "Sometimes I just stay here until I can see things different."

Molly wondered if she could do this, or if he could teach her to do it. He huddled against the water as though it were a skirt.

After a few moments he reached, without explanation, to place his hand on her back. Molly's heart reversed itself—not because she was still afraid, but because she could see the complete darkness in his face and how his eyes emptied toward balance. He looked breathless and without sight. He was young but there was no youth in him, just a vast structure of recollection.

It was then, when he touched her back, that Molly saw in her peripheral vision George Kirby and Joe on either side of the stream. So she knew Lucas had brought back help. She stepped quickly and without hesitation into the pool where Lucas said the crayfish were. As she moved, Joe climbed fast over the rocks.

The man hadn't noticed how quickly Molly stepped away, but when he saw and felt the two men grab his arms he gave out a yell, loud, as though this were his worst betrayal.

"Wait! Let him go," Molly said.

George Kirby dragged the man over the rocks and let him stand. When the man reached for his knife—he didn't reach as though he would harm anyone but just to pick it up because it was his—George grabbed for it.

The man spoke his own name. "Isaac," he said. "Isaac Belcher." His voice was clear, because he was scared.

"He didn't do anything," Molly said. Joe couldn't believe his mother's defense of Isaac. She told them all to get in the car. She said they would have to take care of the sore on his leg. They would take him to the hospital.

Isaac got into the back seat with George Kirby, but before he got in, he put on a hat. He wore it a little to the side in a jaunty fashion, and looked like someone who lived fifty years ago, because it was a felt hat with a dark brim.

Joe drove to the hospital clinic, and Molly tried to make their conversation sound easy. Lucas sat in the front seat between his mother and Joe and looked from one face to the other. "I left my bucket," he said. He didn't know what to think.

Isaac Belcher reminded Molly of a man who used to board with them in Savannah. She mentioned this to her father and asked if he remembered.

"Broadus Smith," said Frank, "but he was older than Isaac."

"I know, but he lived in that room off our porch and sometimes I could peek in to where he sat. If he was in a good mood he'd call me in and give me a piece of hard candy from his jacket pocket. The candy was always covered with lint, but I never mentioned it."

Broadus Smith had never been a young man, or rather Molly could never imagine him young. She knew him for ten years of her early life. He ate meals at their table, and when he wasn't there, Molly missed him and asked the next day where he was.

Mr. Smith took Molly to the county fair each year, where they rode all the rides and saw every freak show. They stood inside the freak tents in an attitude of reverence toward the freaks who explained the reason for their alligator skin or enlarged body part or

double genitals, and when the basket was passed around for dona-
tions, Molly and Mr. Smith always gave a dollar each, so when they
were through with the freak shows they had paid out an extra six-
teen dollars.

"I don't like to go in there," Molly would say when they finished.
Broadus Smith laughed. "But you always beg to go," he said.

Molly begged to do everything. She rode the rides that made her
sick, ate cotton candy, and went to see the animal exhibits with the
prize pig or cow. Each year the winner looked the same.

Mr. Smith returned from the fair with boxes of taffy, which he ate
with Molly in secret until it ran out at Christmastime. And the rest
of the year he kept in his pocket (and in a huge glass jar) hard
candy—sourballs or peppermint sticks.

During the eighth year of his sojourn in their home, Mr. Smith
met a woman and fell in love. Molly couldn't imagine someone that
age being in love. She was twelve and complained when Mr. Smith
spent time with the other woman.

"Of Annabelle?" he said. This wasn't the woman's name. Her
name was Anita, but he called her Annabelle. "You jealous of Annabelle, Molly?"

"Not _jealous_," Molly said. "I just don't think she ought to go with
us to the fair. Nobody ever went _before_."

"Well, honey, she's going." And it was like that from then until
the time he left the house to move in with Annabelle.

Nobody ever figured out if they got married.

Before Broadus Smith moved out, Molly went to tell Annabelle
that Mr. Smith had been married before. Annabelle pretended surprise. "Oh?" she said. "Is that true?" So Molly continued to tell bits
of information she had picked up over the years about Mr. Smith's
wife, then she began to add pieces that were not true, creating a
great fiction which, as she told it, seemed completely right.

After three months, Molly's mother advertised for another
boarder, but whenever anyone applied, Molly said the room had already been filled and she didn't know why her mother hadn't taken
the sign down. Molly didn't want anyone else in that room. She

loved Broadus Smith like an uncle, or even a father or older big brother, and she would save the room until he came back.

But when she visited him at Annabelle's house and saw how happy he was, she stopped thinking about how he would come back. The room stayed vacant until Evelyn Bates fixed it as a guest room, and for a few months during the summer of her sixteenth year Molly moved all her things in there. But it never felt like her own.

That was the summer she met Will, and Broadus Smith got mixed up and forgotten in the maelstrom of her desires. When Molly thought of Mr. Smith in later years, she remembered only two things: his jaunty, dark-brimmed hat and the hard candy.

Isaac stayed in the hospital for four days. His sore healed, and Molly visited and called him several times. Joe went once, because he was curious, and he asked his mother what would Isaac do when he got out. Then he went several more times. Isaac Belcher was not so many years older than Joe.

There is a way of knowing people that is not romance or friendship or family. It is a category that gives rise to a mystery within ourselves. Molly and Joe found it satisfying to speak about Isaac Belcher. It was good to have in their lives the phenomenon of his mysterious presence. They were fascinated. They found out details and spoke of him at the supper table.

"He works for the telephone company, you know," Molly offered. "A lineman, I think."

"He was fired from a couple of jobs because he didn't show up." Joe knew more about Isaac than Molly did.

"He tell you that?"

"Yes."

"What are you talking about?" Lucas took another roll. He wasn't eating anything but bread tonight, but no one noticed.

"He just mentioned the telephone company to me."

"That's the job he has now."

"They're talking about the man you saw in the woods," Franci answered Lucas.

"Oh."

"How old do you think he is?" Molly asked Joe. They ignored Franci and Lucas.

"Twenty-seven. I asked him."

"I think he's weird," Lucas said.

Isaac had come back into the hospital after a few days, because the infection hadn't cleared up. He had tried to go back to work too soon.

"You weren't supposed to walk on it for a while," Molly said.

"You've been real good to me," he told Molly. He lay with the sheet and blanket pulled up under his arms.

"Joe said he would drive if you needed to go somewhere."

"Yeah." His hair was brown and spiritless. "I must've scared you behind the waterfall." He made a gesture that indicated embarrassment.

"You did."

"I'd been out there for four days. Hadn't gone to work or seen anybody."

They spoke about his job, and when the doctor came back, they asked when he could go back to work.

"I have to talk to you," William told Molly. He'd called to ask if he could come over. Molly told Lucas and Franci that their dad would come by "to talk some things over." She asked them not to hang around or interrupt. They both agreed to stay out of the way.

It had been a month since William moved out. The summer vacation had begun, and Franci asked if they were going to the beach. Molly couldn't imagine being at the beach without William, and she tried not to think of him in an intimate way. She even tried to imagine that their intimacy had never been good, that what they had had not been what she wanted, so in that way she let herself be robbed of regular memories.

William came in and walked straight to the den, but Molly suggested they go farther away from where Lucas and Franci were playing. They went into her studio. William hardly ever went in there.

Molly cleared away sections of huge paper. This room had the fragrance of a parlor and the light of a porch. "Sit down, Will." She moved one of her paintings and wished he would comment on it. She wished he would speak of anything but what he had come here for. What he would say would bring a new lash of pain. His whole face said that it would and that it had already done so for him.

"You know I've loved you all my life," he began.

"Yes, I know." Neither of them faced the other.

"You *know* I've loved you." He spoke as though he tried to convince her, but he began to cry. Crying, though, was so unnatural for William that it appeared more like shortness of breath. There were no tears that Molly could see, but his face was unmistakably wet.

"But now there's someone else, and I'm telling you," he spoke fast, "because you stopped asking if there was someone else." William didn't know whether to touch her or not. He shrugged instead.

Molly nodded—one, two, three times. She nodded to keep from speaking. William's hair showed a little grey. She hadn't noticed it before, and wondered how grey her own hair was.

"I'm sorry," said William.

To say he was sorry at such a moment made Molly burn. She wanted to laugh with anger, and did. One short laugh.

"You're sorry! What does that mean!" It was her first outburst. "What about Lucas and Franci? What about Joe?"

"Don't start, Molly." He meant to say more, but she interrupted. He couldn't tell if she had a point he should pay attention to or if she was mad that he had someone else.

"You have no idea, Will. *I'm* with them all the time, and *I* know."

"Don't make me feel guilty, Molly."

"Guilty? This has nothing to do with guilt, Will. Feeling guilty is a *luxury* compared to this. I'm talking about something completely different."

He couldn't answer her. He was convinced she wanted him to feel guilt. His hands were clasped between his legs.

"She young?" Molly wanted to know.

William laughed at himself and at Molly. "Yes." Then he cor-

rected himself. "Not so young." He looked at the floor and got ready
to accuse Molly. "What about you, Molly? You're not exactly *alone*."
He meant Ben McGinnis. Molly had been to dinner with him. "He
stepped in pretty quickly, don't you think?"

Molly shifted her hair away from her eyes. She wore a yellow
shirt she knew he liked and she looked sexy. She hoped he noticed
how sexy she felt. "I'm worried about Joe," she said.

"I see him every day. He seems okay to me. He stays at my place
more than he does here, I think."

This was true, and the thought of the house being without Joe cut
through Molly like a dull blade. There was a wall now, and William
and Molly no longer spoke of anything but themselves and their
own loneliness. "It's too late," Molly said, and William looked at his
watch.

"People are talking about the man you and Lucas saw in the
woods."

"Yes."

"Joe says you went to see him in the hospital." Molly wondered
if Joe had mentioned his own visits with Isaac. They knew him now
as Zack. "That's not such a good idea, Molly. I don't think that's very
smart."

Molly was mad at everything now.

"What's not a good idea," she said, "is to come here and tell me
you love someone else, then give advice about what I should or
should not do."

William was stunned. It hadn't occurred to him that he was giving her advice.

Lucas sat in the carport waiting for them to come out. His face
told what he hoped for, though neither parent noticed it. Franci
straddled her bike, ready to ride off.

William asked Lucas to spend the night at his place on Friday
night, and the suggestion burst open all the wishes they might have
had. Franci rode off on her bike. She rode off fast. Molly called out,
"Franci!" but William said, "Leave her alone."

Last week when Joe drove Franci and Lucas to William's apartment for dinner, they found a note saying, "Eat dinner with Mom." So Joe drove them home, where they found another note telling them, "Go to Dad's tonight. I'll be home at nine." Joe took them to Burger King, where they ate in silence.

When Molly got home they were watching "Cheers" and no one had done any homework. Molly sat until the program was over, then promised it wouldn't happen like that again. She tried to reassure them, but Franci was afraid this kind of thing might happen all her life.

When Frank Bates called the next day, he suggested that he visit them in a week. He wanted to see the Penrys, he said.

Molly had not mentioned anything about William, and she didn't want to do so now. She tried to sound as if she were in a hurry. "I can't talk," she said. "I teach two courses at the Arts Council and I'm late."

"I wanted to come next week," he said.

"We're going to the beach, but I could call you after that."

"No, I mean, I want to come before your beach trip. I told the Penrys I would come soon."

Franci got on the phone. "Papa Frank?"

"Yes, honey."

"A lion fears nothing more than the noise of empty carts."

"I'm glad to know it. I sent you two in my last letter." He had a book from which he lifted his own vague wisdoms, and he wouldn't tell her the name of the book.

"I gave some to Dad," said Franci.

Molly was glad Franci mentioned Will. It made things sound normal.

"We're going to the beach," Franci said.

"I'm coming to see you."

"Yes!" Lucas was on the other phone. "You can sleep in my room."

Molly tried to take back the conversation. "I'll go to the Penrys' for you," she said. "I can go this weekend. I'll call you after I talk with them."

"You don't want me there?" he asked. The children were on the other phones.

"Of course, but I'll call you back," said Molly.

"I don't get it." Lucas spoke from the well of the new portable phone they had bought for Joe.

Molly called the Penrys to say she would make a visit on Friday, but she didn't specify a time.

When she drove up to the house, Tony saw her first and called to tell Louise and Sig. There were five children in the house now: Tony, and a twelve-year-old girl, a boy about fifteen, and two young boys, one three, one five. The girl helped to feed the youngest boy. He ate something that looked like oatmeal, and it had spread in his hair and onto the girl's blouse. The girl's name was Martha, and the little boy was Billy-Bud.

"All but Billy-Bud have been here before," said Louise. Another boy stood behind a chair and wouldn't come out. Sig stayed nearby, but didn't touch the boy or make him move.

Today there would be a new arrival, Sig told Molly. "We didn't know until this morning. She's Carlos' sister." Carlos was the one behind the chair.

Louise motioned for Martha to take Billy-Bud and Carlos to the barn. She asked Jimmy to go with them. Jimmy was fifteen and Louise knew that if Jimmy went, Carlos would want to go too. Not ten minutes had gone by before a truck drove into the driveway.

Carlos was at the barn. They heard him scream as the truck pulled to a stop and a man got out. He walked around to the other side of the truck and told the little girl, Josie, "Come on." Josie wasn't crying, but she had a brooding, dirt-streaked face. She couldn't be more than eight. Her skin was grey, her hair a dark, dark blond and matted.

"She can stay, Eugene," Louise said, her voice stern. "But you have to leave her for a while this time. You can't keep coming back and jerking her from place to place. Leave her and get yourself straight."

Eugene looked undaunted in his dark suit. "Her mama's sick. Real sick." He was trying not to say anything that could be disloyal to anyone.

"Hello, Josie." Louise reached into the truck to lift Josie out. Sig hung back and let Louise handle it. Josie hadn't moved from her seat even though the truck door was open, but she smiled when she saw Louise. She was missing three teeth. "I'm glad you're here, honey." Louise murmured into Josie's ear. She pointed to those on the barn path. "There's Carlos, and Martha's here too." She set Josie on the ground but took her hand. "Your daddy will come see you, but you'll stay with us for now."

Eugene walked around the truck and got in. He didn't wave goodbye until he was sitting behind the wheel, but by then Josie had her back to him. Josie turned to see him just as the truck pulled into the traffic. All the while, Louise talked to her, her voice like the pulse of a heart. Josie made peculiar nervous sounds as she walked beside Louise—throat sounds, like a woods animal.

"Can you stay for supper?" Louise asked Molly.

Molly nodded, so Louise steered her toward the kitchen.

"Good, you can help me cut up some more potatoes and onions. We have enough roast for twenty."

Molly told Louise about Zack Belcher. She thought if Zack had spent his young years here, he would be different now. She wanted to know if they might have a job for him. Louise said to bring him out. "If he can work, he can stay."

Josie sat beside Martha at dinner, and though Martha chattered easily about anything anyone asked her, Josie said hardly a word. Once she asked for more potatoes, and when the sliced, baked apples with cinnamon came around, she asked what that was.

"It's like dessert," Jimmy told her, "only you don't have to eat it last." So Josie smiled and took a baked apple slice. The corners of her mouth began to turn up as she sat there.

It was eight o'clock before Molly left Sig and Louise's. She helped to bathe Josie, Billy-Bud, and Tony. Story-reading was done by Martha, and Tony told a story he made up. Everybody liked his best.

Jimmy stayed in a dormitory room. Molly visited the room and commented on the pennants and pictures he had on his wall. Tony stayed with Jimmy at night, but during the day he had a room of his own.

"He wakes up scared," Louise explained, "but if he sleeps in the room with Jimmy, he's not afraid. It works out." Louise's body assumed the position of staunch tiredness, but her face shone like a broad white ribbon.

Molly could not think of anything but that bright face all the way home.

CHAPTER
FIVE

Franci had the habit of chewing the inside of her mouth but not telling anyone until she created a raw place that made her unable to eat.

"I can't eat that," she said about the meatloaf Molly had made. "It burns my mouth."

"Franci!" It was a reprimand.

"I forgot. Don't fuss at me!"

"You can't keep doing that."

"I know. But *you* bite your fingernails."

"I know."

"And sometimes your fingers get sore."

"I know it."

"What's going to happen to us?"

They were well into summer, and Joe spent so much time with his dad that Franci asked if he was going to move in with him. Joe kept saying he wasn't.

Lucas came in the back door and yelled upstairs. His mother answered from her bedroom. "Are you sick?" he asked, because Molly never sat in her bedroom unless she was sick.

"No. Where've you been?" He had taken off his shoes, and his socks were wet.

"Johnny's. We went to the creek to get crayfish."

"And where did you put them?" She asked as though this were a test question.

"In a bucket. Outside."

Those were the two things she wanted to know. Last week Lucas and Johnny had put crayfish into a sinkful of water and let them crawl out, so Molly found one in the drainer, two on top of the stove, one in the cabinet, and after a few days followed the smell of a dead one under the refrigerator. She had cleaned the refrigerator three times looking for something spoiled.

"Okay."

Lucas crawled onto her lap, tickling her, then leaning back against her. He hadn't done this in a while. Molly wondered what had happened that warranted his sitting on her lap.

"You tired?"

"A little bit." So they both pretended he was doing this because he was tired, and Molly rocked him back and forth for a few moments. Lucas' legs came almost to the floor.

"Lucas?"

He didn't answer.

"What do you think of all this?"

"All what?" He squirmed and she thought he might get up.

"You know." She tried to think of how this had impressed itself upon him. "All this going back and forth from Dad's house to this one."

"It's all right," he said. His grey eyes were a puzzle. He had the expression of someone who has just seen the moon in the middle of the day.

Franci called for Lucas to come downstairs. "Lucas! Your crayfish are loose. They're all over the yard!"

Lucas scrambled up. He didn't want to be seen on his mother's lap.

"Go gather them up," Molly told him, as though she spoke to a shepherd about his sheep.

"Have your separation papers gone through?" Jill asked. She wanted to see Molly get on with her life and she had a particular idea about how she should do this.

"We've signed everything." Molly and Jill had gone shopping and Molly bought a pink shirt that showed off her figure.

"Are you still going out with Ben?"

"Yes."

"Is that all you're going to tell me?"

Molly was dismissive. She changed the subject to Sig and Louise, saying that they were coming to town to talk with the lawyers. She wanted Jill to meet them.

Jill pulled into McDonald's. "Let's eat in the car, okay?"

Molly nodded.

Jill looked for any indication of frivolity in Molly, but her face constricted into a secret security. She recoiled from making any kind of choice. They ate, and Molly stared into her coffee cup.

"I've already told the Penrys you might help them." Molly had asked Jill to think about a feature story with pictures of Sig and Louise and the children at the farm.

"I can't promise anything, Molly. It has to be approved."

"I know." She wondered if Jill had even mentioned it yet to her editor. She didn't push.

"Anyway, I'm trying to ask you about Ben McGinnis."

"There's not much to tell. I'm still *married*, you know."

"You're separated."

"But *here* I'm married." Molly pushed three fingers into the middle of her chest. "In here." She laughed.

Jill agreed with Molly, but it wasn't a pleasant agreement. "You ought to think about it, Molly. I mean, Will is probably going out."

Molly was silent and Jill didn't know whether or not she had made her mad.

"I can't think about that," she said.

That night Ben called to ask when Molly planned to leave for the beach. He said he might come down for a day or two, but his statement about this was a question.

"We don't leave this weekend, but the next," Molly told him.

"Do you mind if I visit you there?" He forced her to answer him. She was wondering about the children. "I guess it's all right."

"Anyway, I have a book for you." He told her the title of the book and said he would wait and bring it to her at the beach. He said it explained difficult concepts in an easy way.

"Easy for you."

"No, no. Things like the Uncertainty Principle."

Molly laughed. They made plans to go out Saturday night, then Ben asked her for Friday night, too. Molly said yes.

She called Jill to say she had two dates with Ben this weekend. "Is that enough?"

"I don't know. Is it?"

Molly spent the whole next day with Jill, wanting to be with a friendly adult rather than with children. Jill had to gather information on an article about urban housing for Sunday's feature section. Molly rode with her into Asheville and nearby small towns. She waited outside office buildings and waited while Jill went to the library. She found a bookstore that had the book Ben had promised to give her. When Jill came out of the library Molly told her, "I found the book Ben talked about and I looked up Uncertainty Principle. One person says it's like trying to measure how fast someone is going by throwing a bicycle at them."

Jill laughed.

Then Molly said, with barely a smile, "It's like asking someone if they still love you."

When they got to the house, William was there. Jill let Molly out. "Call me," she said.

At first it looked as though Will was sitting in the den alone, but Joe was with him and so was Lucas. They had been talking, but when Molly walked in the talking stopped. All their heads were bowed.

"What's the matter, Will?" He was drinking a Coke from the refrigerator.

"We're talking about Joe moving in with me," Will said.

Molly felt a sliding sensation and for a moment could not differentiate among these men. All of them became the same to her.

"Is that what you want, Joe?" Her question came out calm and deliberate. She felt hypnotized by her own voice. "Do you want to live over there?"

"Sort of," he said. He wouldn't commit to anything. "But I wouldn't move out, not really. I would just take more of my things over to Dad's and be there more nights than I am now."

Molly looked again and again for cause and effect. Joe's eyes yielded nothing, and for a moment she thought he looked exactly as he did at one year old in the swimming pool when he stepped off the last step and it was over his head—his eyes open, his mouth no sound. And for Molly to move toward him took so long a time. His hair became springy in the water, his arms came up beside him. Everything ran through her mind, then and now—how it is too late, implications of what can be lost. Molly wanted to lean back into a soft chair of things that could be expected, even predicted. When Joe was a year old, she had moved to lift him out of the deep water. At the time, his kicking and crying could not convince her that he was all right. Now she saw no way to bring his astonished face to the surface. Everything was appalling, clenched. Molly sighed and moved into the sound of her sigh.

"I want you to do what you need to do, Joe," she told him. She was scrounging for love.

William's face, his whole demeanor, looked like rubble. Lucas had not said anything.

Jill called later that night. "What happened? What did Will want?"

"He wants Joe."

"What?"

"Joe wants to move in with him."

"I bet you half expected it, didn't you?"

"Half."

The Penrys came to Molly's house on Thursday at four o'clock. They were late and arrived with a litany of apologies. Jill was already there. She wanted to speak with them about the feature story she might write. Ben came over. Molly wanted everyone to meet Louise and Sig.

But Ben felt awkward, because Joe refused to speak to him. Joe stayed loyal to his father by ignoring Ben and by speaking to everyone else in the language of giving orders.

So Ben stayed out of the way. He waited on the porch, while everyone else stood around the yard.

The yard bristled with birds. One tree had swallowed up hundreds of them, and Franci and Lucas ran toward the base of the tree trying to make them come out. They yelled and waved their arms, and the birds exploded outward and came back. Franci and Lucas made them do it again, and the tree grew loud with impertinence.

After a while, Franci poured lemonade and Ben talked with Lucas about his Little League team. Sig and Louise had brought two children from the farm and everyone made a fuss over them. They had ice cream on the porch, but once Joe followed his mother back to the kitchen. He wanted to say something mean, so he told her he didn't know whether or not he would go to the beach with them. He didn't know if he wanted to go. He said he needed to ask his dad first. And even though he had spoken all of this with authority, he felt poorly concealed. In fact, throughout the afternoon Joe had felt on display.

"It'll be fine with Dad, Joe." Molly dried her hands and turned to face him. "You ask him."

All afternoon the tree stayed busy with the starlings, and Molly imagined that if she opened her mouth wide enough, they might fly in and fill her up.

It was seven o'clock before everyone left. Ben asked to stay for a while. He wanted to see Molly alone, but could think of no way to say he wanted it. He had grown a beard and was nervous about whether or not Molly liked it. The way she looked at him seemed to like it. He motioned for her to sit next to him on the sofa.

Molly wore shorts. Her legs were tanned and long. Her T-shirt was pink and clashed with her hair, but the clash was bold and Ben had already told her he liked it. Molly sat beside him, but was afraid Joe would walk in. She suggested they go for a ride.

As they rode, Molly had the urge to put her head on Ben's shoulder, but couldn't feel the freedom to give that kind of affection. "Joe hates to see me with you," she said. "I can't imagine how that feels— to see your mother with someone else, or your dad."

"I like to think they get used to it," said Ben, "but they probably don't." He stopped the car. It was dark enough now to see the constellations. Ben pointed out the North Star to orient Molly. He placed his arm around her shoulder and said something to make her laugh. It was when he made her laugh that Molly thought she loved him.

But right now, with his arm around her and his mouth soft, she knew he would kiss her. The surge that came was one that Molly associated with fear. His mouth, his tongue. She kissed him back, the birds going inside her chest. He pulled away, so Molly kissed him again, hungry—*don't go*—her tongue sinking into his mouth— *don't go*. She didn't know what was happening.

When she looked again at Ben's face, he said, "Well!" He seemed amazed, but not surprised.

Ben had seen Molly even before she entered his classroom. He had seen her alone at concerts and once at a play. Each time she had come to those places alone, so it was with disappointment that he learned she was married. He hadn't known she was a painter until that first time she showed him her notebook. Since then she had finished two paintings—one of a lunar eclipse, and another of girls sitting on the porch of a big house. She titled this last *The Pleiades*.

> If given enough time, what kind of girls would the Pleiades be? How long would it take those sisters to grow up and become more than daughters? How long will it take me?

Molly showed the paintings to Ben and asked if she could use one of them as a class project. Ben told her that he couldn't give her credit for a project that didn't involve research and a written report. Later, he was afraid he had said something terribly wrong. He called her house the next day.

"Molly Hanner, please," he said, when a young voice answered.

"Mama! Telephone! Some *man*!"

Molly came to the phone. "Hello?"

"Hello."

"Hello!" She knew who it was.

"This is Ben."

"Yes."

"I wanted to change my mind and say that you could work on a project that had both a painting and a short written explanation." He didn't back all the way down.

"Thank you." Her pleasure was unmistakable.

"Who is it?" asked Lucas. He'd been watching a TV program where people were called on the air and presented with questions, and if everything was answered correctly the contestant won either a boat or a jeep. "Who *is* it?" he asked again. Molly pointed a finger at him like it was a pistol.

"One of Kepler's Laws, maybe," she said into the phone, and it sounded like an answer to a question. It sounded like a *right* answer, and Lucas could not be quieted.

"Did we get the *boat*?" he screamed.

"Lucas! Shhh!" She didn't even try to guess what he meant.

"Maybe we can discuss this next week," she told Ben. "I'll come in early."

Ben McGinnis couldn't sleep that night.

Lucas stopped pulling at his mother's shirt. "I thought we were going to win," he said, disappointed.

"What are you talking about?"

"A program I saw."

"Oh, Lucas. Nobody ever wins that stuff."

"Yes, they do," he told her, disappointed now in his mother. "Some people do."

A strong force was gathering under the conscious surface of their life, and though Molly didn't know the source of its fury, she knew it lay in Lucas' ability to hope for a boat or a jeep.

"I know. Sometimes they do," she said.

The shadow that lay on Molly was like a cargo she carried. She wanted to be with Ben McGinnis, but she hadn't thought herself available for such imprudence. She was taking note of something. "Take note," her mind said. But sometimes she only had the pieces, like the way she remembered "anymore" and thought of "I don't love you." Or the way she knew an entire psalm by thinking "I shall not want."

"I can't figure this out," Franci said about her new swimsuit. The long straps were supposed to wrap around her in a complicated way. Only ten more days until the beach. Joe said he would go with them, and they had begun to plan what to take. Franci put the suit on over her clothes and tried to make it fit. Lucas came in while she worked on it.

"I can do it." He took one strap and wrapped it a certain way, then took another and did the same. It wasn't exactly right, but it looked good. Franci liked it.

Molly went to Lucas' room to ask what clothes he would pack. She wanted to wash his clothes before the trip. He gave her nine T-shirts and four pairs of shorts.

"What about underwear?"

"I'll wear some."

"You'll need more than one pair, Lucas. We're staying a week."
She saw that he had some of Joe's tapes in his room.

"Does Joe know you have those?"

"Not yet."

"I think I'd tell him if I were you."

"I will." It sounded like a promise to be carried out sometime in the future.

Louise called and her voice was excited as she told Molly how Jill's editor had decided to do a feature article on them. The lawyers were hopeful. Her voice had more than gladness in it, it had an expression of being restored. The restricted scope of their life had grown larger, and Molly was left with a strong temperature around her.

When she hung up the phone, she stood in the hallway and heard Franci and Lucas talking in Franci's room.

"They're not going to start hating each other like Johnny's parents did," said Franci.

"Johnny's parents don't hate each other," Lucas defended Johnny.

"Yes, they do. Johnny's mama's always saying how bad he treated her and how mean he is."

"But they didn't used to be that way."

"I know, but they are now."

Molly didn't realize Joe was in the room until he spoke. "I remember when I was little and asked Dad if they'd ever get divorced."

"What'd he say?"

"He just laughed. They both laughed whenever I said it, because I usually asked when they were arguing about something. They promised they never would."

"Will they?" Lucas.

"Will they what?" Franci.

"Get divorced."

"It's as good as done." Joe.

That night Molly lay flat and thought of herself as a geometry of straight lines against an expanse of white sheet. When she was a child, her mother would sometimes make up the bed with her in it, or else Molly might jump into the bed she was making. Her mother would snap the sheet in the air and make it fall around her. She would lift it several times, bringing it down slowly, the soft light cotton landing on Molly's arms and legs at different moments. She'd let it settle, then whip it up again, and Molly could feel the air curving in and out of the place where she lay. Her arms, she could see her mother's arms lift in a grand sweep and what she felt did not belong to her regular life. She knew that even then. Nor did it belong to anything she could recognize at that age. It belonged to somewhere in-between, and sometimes in this place Molly became a strange personal friend, a native version of herself.

She fixed her mind on the window where she could see a thin sickle of new moon, but before she was good asleep, Lucas cried out. He still woke at night with bad dreams. It had been two weeks since he had had one.

"Tell me the dream," Molly said.

"No."

"Say it out loud, Lucas. It won't be so big in your mind. Say it and it gets smaller." She wished he would talk more.

"It was about Dad."

"What was it? Just say it, Lucas."

"That he was sick, like Grandmama. I dreamed about the funeral, like hers."

"Oh, honey. Your mind just mixed up those things. Daddy's not sick at all." And Molly suggested that Lucas spend this weekend with Will. "We'll call tomorrow and tell him you want to come over on Saturday. You and Joe can both spend the night."

That sounded fun to Lucas. It sounded manly. "Yeah."

"Now," and she tucked him in, "this weekend you can be with Dad and next weekend we'll go to the beach." She wanted his life to sound like a fun thing.

"What day do we go?" He already knew but wanted to hear it said.

"A week from Saturday."

The next afternoon Franci brought Fire for her mother to see. He wasn't red anymore, but a dark grey color. "Caroline said she'd take care of him while we're at the beach." The fox was still kept in the garage. He was big enough now to be let go. Even with all its domestication, the fox had a wild look. Franci renewed herself in its wildness. "And Joe said to tell you he and Lucas are staying at Dad's tonight."

The house would seem empty without even one male figure around. "We should go out," Molly suggested. "See a movie."

A year ago Franci would've leapt at this suggestion, but now she was almost thirteen and didn't respond to her mother in the same way.

"What movie?"

"Your choice."

"Okay then. *Rocky III*." Franci spoke with the sureness of someone who has already seen the movie and knows it is still showing. But it was with no small regret that Molly imagined her night ahead in the movie theater with the sleek, stupid-talking Sylvester Stallone.

CHAPTER SIX

"You know what my team does?" Lucas interrupted Joe, who had turned halfway around in the car to talk to Papa Frank about baseball. Papa Frank arrived on the four-thirty flight. He had called to say he wanted to be there for two or three days and that he would come before they left for the beach. So Molly told him about Will.

"What does it do?"

"We play ten games and whoever wins the most gets to play in the championship." He yelled the word championship, so Molly said shhh, but immediately regretted saying it. Franci sat with her whole side pressed against Papa Frank.

"How many have you won so far?"

"Three."

"How many have you played?"

"Six, but one was forfeited."

"Well, that's pretty good."

"I know it." Then Lucas said, "Dad lives at another house," blurting out what was on everybody's mind.

"I know it," said Papa Frank, and Lucas looked relieved. Joe spoke again about baseball.

"Molly." Frank Bates came into her room after everyone had gone to bed. "I want to say this, just this one thing."

"I know what you're going to say."

"You might not."

"Don't tell me everything will work out. I know you think it will, but don't tell me that."

"I can tell you that your mother and I had a time like this. And that we waited it out."

"People don't wait it out anymore. Nobody does that." Molly didn't want to hear about her mother or what her parents had done.

"Remember that doll I made for you?"

Molly said she did.

"I started working on it the day I found that letter in the hall table. I read the first few lines, then put it away. I wonder sometimes if Evelyn wanted me to see it, because she put the letter in the drawer of the table and even though I never looked there, it was still a likely place to find it."

Her father wore a collarless shirt and Molly hardly ever saw him in that kind of attire. "But there were other signs," he said. "She found ways of avoiding sitting in the same room with me, and she didn't get irritated at things that had made her mad before.

"I started to read magazines just so I could sit in the same room with her, and I started to think of all the times she couldn't have loved me at all. Then one night, she said, 'Frank,' and I looked up from a *National Geographic* I had read three times. 'Frank, we have to talk.'"

Molly looked at her father, because he suddenly laughed and she thought he might change the subject.

"If a woman says she wants to talk," he said, "it usually means she's going to make some statement about how unhappy she is. But what Evelyn said was more like confession. She told me about Jeff Foster. I knew him. But she kept calling him 'Jeffrey' so I imagined she must not know him very well. She said how sorry she was and wanted me to forgive her." And though Frank didn't say it, he remembered how her voice sounded like it came down a long tube.

"I don't know what this has to do with me," Molly said.

"This is the part I want to tell you, Molly. When she told me, right at first, I was glad she said it, because I didn't know if I wanted to be married to her anymore. That's how I felt. That's all I'm saying." His peregrinations asked for a complicity that Molly didn't want to give.

"And I got up from my chair and said, 'I'm going to bed now. You sleep down here.' It felt appropriate to say that—like something out of a B movie. I think I seemed dashing and handsome going off up the stairs. We never mentioned it again." This was all Frank Bates told her, but he said goodnight and leaned to kiss her cheek. When he did, Molly could smell his particular odor of age.

That night Molly dreamed about her mother, of an actual time in the hospital room when they looked out the window at the court-yard trees. Sadness bloomed in them both like an odd flower, and even the sharp edges of shadow on the grass made them cry. Then, as can happen in dreams, the scene became one of night, and a wash of moonlight came in onto her mother's bed. They were still looking out the window as a shooting star fell from the constellation of Taurus. It was a moment they both recognized as an opportunity for wishing, but neither of them knew what to wish for.

"What're you planting?" Franci came out to see what Papa Frank was doing in the garden. He would visit with Sig and Louise later, but now he planted bulbs for Molly. Papa Frank knew everything about gardens. He considered himself an amateur naturalist.

Franci wore a shirt with huge orchids on it, and white shorts that fit tightly around her bottom. She was lovelier than she knew. She was barefoot and her hair had not been combed.

"You just wake up?"

She sat beside him and offered a cinnamon roll out of the sack she carried. "Um-hm." She would tell him a secret.

Whenever she approached him with quietness, she was thinking how to tell him something. Once she told him about the way she divided everything into separate genders: plates were feminine, and rims of cups. Everything with sharp angles was masculine—

windowpanes and clocks, bookcases. Sometimes, though, a thing might have a feminine shape and a masculine color, like a dark red armchair, or a pocket in a pair of black pants.

"Fred Jarelson kissed me two days ago." Her secrets were becoming different now.

"He did?"

"Yes."

"Did you like it?"

"No." He waited for the lie to expose itself. "I liked it some."

"Well, I used to like it when your grandmother kissed me." He handed her some bulbs and a bag of topsoil. He dug a shallow hole and spoke of the dramas found in each layer. He encouraged her to sit quietly beside him.

"*The grasshopper sings its song and puts the cuckoo to silence. It dies in oil and revives in vinegar. It sings through the burning heat.*"

In the early part of his life Frank Bates might have been drawn to a girl's physical beauty, but now he felt turned by a gesture or a tone of voice that invoked a memory. And to have Franci beside him made a memory surface, so he shifted himself, hoping to find whatever it was.

"Is he going to kiss you again?"

"I don't know." She looked shocked that he had asked such a personal question.

The air had already begun to steam in the June heat. Papa Frank pointed out a mountain butterfly named after a spider beause the pattern on its wings resembled a web.

"I hate my name," said Franci. She could tell him anything.

"You're named after me. I'm named Francis too."

"Don't you just *hate* it?"

"I used to, but I like being called Frank."

"I hate mine. I hate all of it." She got up as though she might do something about it. "C'mon," she said. "I want to show you something."

"What is it?"

"It's a fox. Didn't Mama tell you?" Frank followed along behind her to the garage. "But there's only one left now. I named him Fire. He's the only one I named."

They lifted the garage door and closed it quickly. The fox ran loose.

"You need a pen for it," Papa Frank said.

"Could *you* build one? If you build one, he won't run away."

"I guess I could, but you can't keep him forever."

"Why not?"

The fox stuck its sharp face from behind the freezer. He looked diminished by the time in the garage. "You'll have to let him go soon, Franci. Look at him."

They exchanged a look of apology and Franci held her mouth in a smile, much the way someone does who has had novocaine and the smile is dead on one side. Then she angled under the garage door to answer her mother calling to them from the house. Molly suggested they go in to Asheville with her.

"I'm taking paintings to Asa. He said to bring them before I go to the beach." Franci didn't want to go. She wanted to stay with Papa Frank, but he wanted to go with Molly.

"Papa Frank's going to build a pen for Fire."

The road to Asheville ran west and curved through a row of hills. For a mile or two the stretch of road had deep ruts and potholes, but then it eased onto a highway which let them ride without thinking of anything.

Franci didn't want to sit in the back seat with her mother's paintings, so she crowded in front between the two of them.

"Are we taking these to Mr. Caldwell?"

"Yes."

"Will he keep them for the museum?"

"I hope so."

"Can we stop for ice cream?"

"I thought you were going with Fred Jarelson to get ice cream this afternoon."

"Uh-uh. Yogurt."

"Fred Jarelson, huh?" Papa Frank stared straight ahead to let her know he wouldn't give away her secret. "Is this somebody new?"

"He's the best soccer player in school," Molly boasted for Franci, "and you should see them together. He's crazy about Franci."

"Mama!"

"He follows her everywhere."

"Mama!" Franci looked pleased to be spoken of as irresistible and to be for a moment the center of her mother's and Papa Frank's life.

Frank saw Asa Caldwell as an impressive, intellectual kind of man. He wore a very expensive sport coat, and he inspected each canvas closely. He liked the tones of indigo Molly had used to intensify light around a shadowy place.

He very quickly decided on the ones he would keep, and as he did he spoke to Frank Bates, saying something about each one. It seemed inappropriate to make these remarks to Frank, but Asa thought he ought to say something. Molly had introduced her father as a newspaperman, and Frank was writing down Asa's remarks. For Asa, the attraction of having someone write down what he said was hard not to indulge.

On the way home Frank read to Molly what Asa Caldwell had said. Like any good newspaperman, he had taken mental notes along with what he had written down.

"A sensory projection and rich, impassive strength," Frank read. "Your images do not fade under scrutiny." Molly was glad he wrote it down for her, because she could never remember exactly the way Asa said it.

Franci sat in the back seat on the way home. She'd wanted to sit in front between them again, but Papa Frank wasn't comfortable that way, so she sat in back and imagined how Fred Jarelson might kiss her, if they were older. She slipped into daydream.

She imagined the voices in the car were those of her father and mother, and that everything was regular. She imagined this deeply enough to put her to sleep, knowing, not consciously, that a wish can come so hard that it turns to dream—a fluctuating, grey world where anything can be true. She didn't wake up until she felt the car move onto the gravel of her own driveway.

"Are we home?" she asked.

The decision to build the pen was definite.

Papa Frank agreed to do it, if the children would help. "We can build it in one day," he promised. He said this to Joe, because he knew Lucas and Franci would be willing.

But Joe surprised them by being more than willing. He suggested he spend the night at home and that they get up early. He wanted his mother to fix a huge breakfast, and he went with Papa Frank to choose the boards and nails and wire. Franci made the decision about where the pen should go. Lucas spent the day making a shelter for the fox out of an old doghouse.

Molly made breakfast at seven o'clock and then watched them from her studio as they worked. It was nearly five when they asked her to look at what they had done. The fox was already inside the pen, running from corner to corner to smell its boundaries.

Joe stayed at home for the next few days. Loose air dissipated around his head. He asked if his dad could come over to look at the fox pen, and Molly said he could.

Molly had seen William only when he came to pick up Lucas and Franci at the house, or else she saw him from a distance someplace, and he didn't see her. Whenever she saw him, she turned away because she didn't know how—and this was strange—she didn't know how to speak to him in public.

William did not come by the house, but called about ten.

"I was wondering where Joe was," he said. "Will he be staying with me tonight?"

"I don't think so," said Molly. She found it difficult sometimes not to use an endearment. Sometimes on the phone Will called her "babe." "Okay, babe," he'd say, "tell Joe I called." And sometimes Molly said, "Bye, hon," and when she hung up would feel the kind of random destructiveness that comes with loss. They didn't slip into endearments so much anymore. Both of them, at some great price, kept their dignity.

On Thursday night before they left for the beach, Frank Bates noticed the first unmistakable symptom. He was sitting in the den around midnight. Everyone had gone to bed. He had gone to bed too but couldn't sleep so got up to watch TV. He thought Joe was already home, and he was alarmed when he heard the key in the door.

"It's just me," Joe said, coming in heavy-eyed and speaking too loud for sobriety. Frank reminded him that everyone was asleep, and Joe headed for the bathroom.

When Joe was a little boy he had been quiet and obedient. He took long naps and was an easy child to take care of. That's how his mother described him. But when he turned fourteen, he began to hang around with boys who never studied. They roamed the woods and creeks, and came into the house with absurd hilarity, wearing no shirts and eating all the food. Their skinny chests and wiry arms turned visibly into bodies of raucous men.

"I'll get you something to eat," Frank offered. "Are you hungry?"

"I don't want anything," Joe said. Frank ignored him and brought in cheese and crackers, with one hard roll left over from supper.

"I don't want your mother to see you like this," he told Joe. "Where've you been, and where'd you get the stuff you've been drinking?"

"Andrew's. We sat around in his room. I didn't think I had so much. Andrew is _so_ lucky, man."

"You know, Joe," Papa Frank said, "there's a chance things might work out."

"Naw," Joe said. The room seemed to widen, become stellar in its proportions. Joe swooned. "I don't think there's a chance in hell of that." Frank took some crackers and cheese, and Joe ate the roll. They watched comedians on TV and ate more out of camaraderie than hunger. But before Frank went to bed, he said, "No more of this, Joe." He meant the drinking. "I mean it."

"I know." Joe's voice was contrite, but there was no conviction in it.

The next afternoon Ben came over. Papa Frank had left that morning. He rented a car and would spend a few days with Sig and Louise before going home. Molly sat in a lawn chair outside her studio, sunning. She wore a bright red swimsuit and had a sketch pad on her lap. She glistened with oil and looked shiny and wet. When Ben came around the corner of the house, he whistled at her.

"Lucas and Johnny said you were working back here."

"Just this." Molly held up rough sketches, which Ben only half looked at. "What's the matter?" Molly hadn't seen this expression before. She thought something had happened. They went into her studio.

"Last night I couldn't sleep or read." It sounded like a confession. "And I realized it was because I think so much about you." There was more in his mind to say. "I've never seen you asleep." He spoke sadly. His mind fumbled and he took off his glasses. A blue artery was visible at his throat and his hands were curved into a half-fist. Molly wanted to touch him, but first she spoke in a heavy, overemphasized voice.

"There's never been anyone but William." His mouth was just above her slick shoulder. "But I'll tell you something," she said. "I've wanted you to say this to me. I've thought how you might say it."

He buried his face in her hair and moved his hands over her back. He kissed her. He had so many tongues. How many tongues did he have? He put his hand on her breast, and a flickering penciled line of confusion broke across them as they heard the front door slam. Johnny and Lucas came in.

"Mom!" Lucas' voice was urgent with boredom. "We can't think of anything to do!" He tried to open the studio door and yelled. "Hey! This door is *locked*!"

Ben unlocked it to let the boys in.

"What is there to *do*?"

Molly mentioned three things, but they hated all that she named. Ben suggested they throw the baseball in the yard. They assumed he offered himself in the suggestion and ran to find an extra glove. Molly petted his soft brown head like an animal's and trembled with the way he had made her want him.

"Mom? Can Johnny go with us to the beach?"

"No, honey. Not this year."

"But last year you said maybe he could go with us *this* year. Remember?"

Molly grew angry at the implication that this year was the same as last, and she answered Lucas so severely that Lucas closed his eyes as though he had been struck.

They were on the porch waiting for Jill to come over for lunch. She was bringing Dan, so it was a serious move. Midday locust sounds rose from the long cove at the end of the street, and frogs were unrelenting as they roared from the water gaps near the house.

She could see Lucas on the low swing that hung from the oak in the front yard. He waited for Johnny to come back out. He would have to tell Johnny he couldn't go to the beach with them this year. His feet worked, without vigor, to swing himself back and forth.

Molly saw that he was barefoot and wanted to tell him to put on his shoes, but she let it go. The rags of sunlight that came into the yard had a harsh whiteness, but a milder light lay under the tree where Lucas swung. And when the locusts stopped for a moment, the hush Molly heard felt like a reprimand. So she called across to the rope swing and told Lucas that she would take them to the water slide this afternoon and that he could ask Johnny to go.

When Jill drove up, Molly recognized Dan in the seat beside her. She recognized him as a friend of Will's, and she understood something about Jill when she saw him.

"What have you done, Jill?" Molly asked when lunch was over and no one else was around.

"What do you mean?"

"I mean, as soon as I saw Dan Berry, as soon as I saw him in the car and he came onto the porch, I recognized him and knew you'd been keeping something from me. How could you do that?" She tried to be careful of any gesture that might disclose her own intransigence.

"What could I have said, Molly? What could I have *told* you? I never spoke directly to Will, just heard things through Dan."

"I want to *hear* what you knew. I want to hear it now."

Franci had already interrupted them twice to say she wanted somebody to take her to the mall. "You're not going to that mall again," Molly said. She spoke crossly almost every day now. Joe was spared her bad humor only because he wasn't at home much. "You can *forget* about it," she told Franci, and she heard Franci tell Lucas to "leave Mama alone."

"Jill, what I'm imagining is probably much worse than anything you're going to tell me."

"Okay, but let's don't talk here. Let's go to your studio."

They walked silently to the studio and Jill sat in a chair while Molly stood.

"It was about a year ago that Will told Dan he was afraid the two of you wouldn't make it. He was unhappy, and he was falling in love with somebody else."

"Which came first?" Molly tried not to look surprised or angry. "I mean, did he fall in love and decide we wouldn't make it? Or did he decide we wouldn't make it and fall in love?" She kept her face like a white surface.

"Who knows, Molly? How can you ask that?"

"I can ask anything I want, Jill. I'll ask this: what kind of friend would let everything go wrong like that?"

"I didn't do that, Molly. You're just wanting to blame somebody. You're glad you might be able to blame this on me."

"What do you expect me to think? You knew this and didn't tell me."

"Hell, Molly, you knew everything I knew. You just didn't look at it. And so I was caught in the middle. It wouldn't have made any difference if I had said something to you."

"What did Dan say?"

"Just that Will wasn't happy."

"What else?"

"You mean about Carol?"

"Did you know about that?"

"Nobody knows that but Will."

Molly hadn't taken her eyes from Jill, but Jill turned away. "Anyway, Molly, I wasn't sure what you were doing when you took that course with Ben McGinnis. Will wasn't sure either."

Molly didn't offer any explanation. She liked pretending a private indifference.

"Molly," Jill said, "I really hate you for putting me in this spot."

"Well, I hate you for being in it."

It was three o'clock when the water slide crowd arrived—Lucas, Johnny, Johnny's brother, Franci, Caroline, and one child Molly had never seen. The extra child was named Elaine and she lived two streets over.

"Her mother said she could go," Franci said. Molly called to check. The little girl was only four, but Caroline said they would take care of her. Elaine wore a swimsuit that emphasized the downward curve of her stomach and her eyes shone with excitement. She said she didn't need any help, that she had been to the water slide at least fifty times and that she would be in the first grade after next year.

They piled into the car for a thirty-minute ride. Elaine sat in front on Caroline's lap. The boys sat in back. Johnny's brother was fourteen and surly and embarrassed to be with all these younger kids. He asked if Joe were going.

"I thought Joe was going," he said, but got into the car anyway. He brought along his skateboard to be different.

"Joe went somewhere with Andrew." Lucas allied himself with his brother by knowing his whereabouts.

Johnny's brother was called Meatball, and though Molly had

heard his real name, she didn't remember what it was, so she called him Meatball too. He liked the name, because he thought it sounded like a football player.

Ben drove up to the house just as they were leaving. He asked if they had room for one more. He didn't even ask where they were going, but climbed into the back seat, moving Meatball away from the coveted window and making him groan at the inconvenience.

"Will you go down the water slide with us?" Franci asked Ben. She never addressed him directly by his name, but just called him "you," though when she asked her mother about him she would say, "Is Ben coming over?" or "Are you going out tonight with Ben?" None of them knew what to call him in person.

"Should I?"

"Yeah," Meatball said. It was a challenge. So the moment they arrived at the water slide, Ben stripped off his shirt and shoes and raced them for the slide. Molly wore a bathing suit under her clothes but didn't tell anyone because she hadn't decided yet if she would participate. She slipped her clothes off and put them in the trunk of the car. Elaine seemed reluctant to go with the others and held tightly onto Molly's hand.

"Aren't you glad I came?" Ben said as he raced with the boys toward the slide. Molly raced too, but she had to stop to tie the laces on Elaine's shoes. Everyone passed her.

"I don't know yet," she yelled. But she was more than glad to have Ben. He could bring bright commotion to paltry moments.

CHAPTER
SEVEN

Joe sat in the front seat beside his mother, mad because she wouldn't let him drive to the beach. William's absence was clear in everyone's mind and Molly tried to think of some easy way to mention him. She pictured how she might say something to ease the tension, but hadn't thought of anything when Franci said, "Remember how Dad liked Jay's Barbeque and always wanted to stop there?"

Nobody ever wanted to stop when William suggested it.

"We could stop there for lunch," Molly said.

"Ga, Mom." Joe turned to look at Franci. "It doesn't seem right to stop somewhere he always wanted to stop when now he's not even *with* us."

"I want to," said Franci. "I remember he *always* said it. We just never liked barbeque before."

"Why is everybody saying 'remember'? He's not *dead*. We're talking about him like he's *dead*." Lucas spoke out the window. "Anyway, I don't want any. I *hate* barbeque."

"*I* do. I like it now."

"You like it now?" Joe was the only one who ever challenged Franci. "Since when?"

"I've had some," she told him. "You think I haven't had any."

"Where?"

"At Fitch's."

"Yuk!" said Lucas. "Somebody told me old Mr. Fitch had to have a operation in his *stomach*."

"Well," said Molly. The moment she hoped for was lost. "Maybe we could stop on the way home. We'll just get something at Hardee's."

"I don't care," said Joe. He imagined he sounded agreeable. "Do whatever you want." Then after a few moments Joe said, "Mom, why don't you ever object to the kind of food we eat?" It was an accusation. "Other parents object to the way *their* kids eat."

"What do you mean?"

"You know. You bring home Doritos and cookies and stuff."

"You *ask* for it." She was getting tired of being cooped up in the car with them and wondered if Joe would be this cross all the way to the beach.

"But you never *say* anything about it," said Franci. Molly imagined they had been discussing her leniency among themselves.

"Yeah," said Lucas, "and another thing—why don't you make me brush my teeth?"

"Don't you brush your teeth?"

"Not much."

"Well, you *should*." Molly tried to sound firm.

"I just wondered why you let us do that." Joe looked at his mother as though she were on the witness stand and this answer was important to the case.

She turned her head to the back seat. "Lucas, let me see your teeth." He gave her a wide grin. "They *are* yellow."

"Mom! Watch where you're going!" Franci yelled. "I don't brush *my* teeth either."

"You *don't?*"

Joe looked so unhappy—as if something had escaped him and he would not have the chance to get it back.

"I'll tell you *one* thing," she told them all, "you'd better start brushing your teeth!" They sat back, relaxed. "And if you want to curb the kinds of food we eat, that's *fine* with me. Let's stop at the truck stop that has all those vegetables. That funny hillbilly place."

It was a truck stop William liked, though no one mentioned it. They just said yes, it would be a good place to stop, as though they were deciding something about their eating habits in a firm and drastic way.

"We can eat vegetables," Franci said. She had recently learned to like vegetables and was proud of it.

An hour passed before they saw the sign advertising a place that offered a chance for ruby mining. Franci saw the sign first and suggested they stop.

"You mean now?" Molly asked.

"It's just two miles off the exit," Joe said.

Lucas said he wanted to go.

"You've never *done* that?" Joe asked in a tone designed to make everyone defensive.

"*I've* done it before. That's why I want to now."

"I *never* have," said Lucas.

So Molly turned off the highway, hoping the excursion might change everyone's mood.

A stream two miles down the road had a stand where a man sold buckets of mud for a dollar, and he gave each person a screen to pan for rubies. Joe had his own money and bought two buckets.

"It's a *dollar* for a bucket of *mud*?" Lucas asked. "For *one bucket*? We should get a *hundred* buckets for that."

Molly bought Franci and Lucas a bucket each and one for herself. "This might be fun," she said. She wore jeans and a T-shirt, her hair was pulled back into a full bush, and bright gold-red wisps fell around her face.

The man gave them flat screens and Franci squatted near the stream to let water wash off the mud and gravel. They searched for rubies, but they were quiet as they searched.

"I didn't get one," Lucas announced, saying it as though he mentioned success instead of failure. He poured more mud over his screen.

"I think I found something," said Franci. She fingered through the gravel softly. She wanted so much to be the one who found something valuable.

Lucas reached over to see what she had. "That's not anything. It's not even *red*. That's just a rock."

"Sometimes you can't tell." Franci lifted it out and placed the rock on the ground beside her. "It *might* be something." She would keep it, in case.

"I didn't find one." Lucas poured more mud onto his screen.

"You're going too fast," Franci warned. "You'll waste it all."

"No, I'm not. There's nothing *there*."

Franci held up another rock. "See?" she said. "But I don't know if it's real yet." She measured out her mud very carefully, pouring it over her screen as if she were serving a delicious sauce and didn't want to waste a drop.

Joe finished his first bucket and offered to share his second with Franci. She had a small pile of gravel saved next to her. "If you find something though," he said, "it's half mine." He smiled to show he wouldn't hold her to it.

"I believe I've found something," Molly said. She brought several pieces to the man in the shed. She had entered the ruby panning with gratitude, and had found something—one rock not like the others. It felt greasy to touch.

The children followed to see what the man would say. It was a ruby, he told them. The biggest one anyone had found in months. Molly brightened, though she had hoped one of the others would find something. She offered to let them have it. Joe said she should keep it, so she told him he could drive the rest of the way to the beach, and Lucas could ride in the front seat.

Franci kept the rocks she found and didn't ask the man in the shed if they were real. Later she could say she'd found something and thought it was a ruby, but she wasn't sure yet if it was real or not. "If that was *mine*," Franci said to her mother, "I would put it on a chain and make a necklace out of it."

"Hint, hint," Joe teased. They went back to the car in a different mood.

"*Love conquers everything*," Franci said, but it didn't seem long enough, so she added, "*The words freeze in your mouth and you will make ice on Mount Etna.*"

"What?" Joe shook his head at her, but it was with pleasure. Being able to drive them somewhere made him feel like an adult, and so he had the patience an adult was supposed to have.

Molly played Twenty Questions and I Spy with Franci, then fell asleep with her head in Franci's lap. She pretended she had suddenly been made into a child, and these were her parents driving her somewhere.

"I don't want this," Molly had said to her father, when she heard that Lucas had asked him to build a tree house. Papa Frank had suggested that William build it for them. "I mean, I don't want Will over here all the time, in the yard and house." It didn't seem fair. "I hate that."

"Only for one or two weekends, Molly." Frank Bates spoke without patience. "This is not for you or for Will. It's just that those kids need something other than just going to supper with Will on Wednesday nights. You know?"

They chose the tree and a specific nest of branches where the tree house would go. Molly knew it would be good for them.

What Molly didn't know was what to expect anymore. As a child she always awoke with excitement, expecting something to happen. Even into adulthood this habit persisted. Molly woke thinking something was promised to her. "You wish for too much," her mother warned, but she meant the warning as a kindness. As Molly grew older, it seemed that what was promised was not something she would receive, but something she would need to give.

The other thing she did not know was this: how William felt every time he came into the house, seeing the tulipwood table with its delicate striations and the disparate objects laid on it. She didn't know that there were nights when the absence of his family loomed like a presence around him and that on those nights William wept without restraint, as a child does who has stayed up long past his bedtime. And sometimes when he called and asked to speak to Molly, Lucas answered the phone.

"She can't come to the phone right now. She's taking a bath." Then Lucas said he had to go, because his favorite TV show was starting. He hung up the phone.

"Goodbye, Lucas," William said to no one.

Molly had reserved two rooms.

"We don't need both rooms," Joe said. He used the same tone William would have used if he had been there. "Why don't we get one with two double beds? Lucas can sleep with me."

"Let's keep it this way, Joe." She didn't want to say how much she needed to have a room alone. He didn't want to say how he wished for them to be together in one room.

"It'll cost too much." He had the look of someone who wished he had never grown up. He didn't know how to object.

"I *want* it this way," Molly confided to him in a whisper.

"Lucas takes up the whole closet," Franci complained from the other room.

Franci had thrown Lucas' suitcase onto the bed, but she hadn't meant for it to open and scatter all his clothes.

"What's the matter with you, Franci?" Joe came in to quieten them.

"I'm going to stay in the room with Mama." Her voice grew shaky.

"No, you're not. Now let's unpack and go to the beach. You *too*, Lucas."

"You can't boss me around."

Joe didn't know if Lucas was talking to Franci or to him. He pulled out his swimsuit and suggested they go to the beach even before they unpacked. Franci filled the drawers with her clothes.

"Mama always makes us do this first," she said, and made the drawer look neat so her mother would like it. Lucas turned his back to undress, but Franci saw his bottom and told him so. "I can see everything." She waited until she could have the bathroom to put on her own swimsuit.

"I don't care." Lucas wiggled quickly and got a beach towel. He handed one to Franci.

"I'm not using that one." She reached for a hotel towel and said she wanted to "save" hers.

"What for?" Lucas asked, but Joe said to leave her alone and they walked out. Franci hurried. She wanted to catch up with them. She didn't want to go to the beach by herself.

"Is Mama coming?" she yelled, trying to get them to wait. They were almost to the beach. Lucas walked with his towel wrapped around his neck, and he held both ends the way Joe was doing. He stepped exactly the way Joe stepped. "*Is* she?" Franci always felt left out when they walked that way together.

"I don't know."

They could see Molly on the balcony of her room. She yelled some instruction to them and they waved, pretending they heard her.

Franci ran straight into the ocean. "This water's *cold*," she said.

"You complain too much," Joe told her. He was still mad at his mother.

"She complains all the time," said Lucas. "She complains about *me*!"

Joe waded up to his knees and Lucas went all the way in, but shivered.

"See?" Franci then motioned for Lucas to come with her, and they went toward a man sitting on the beach surrounded by rows and baskets of shells. The man sat in a beach chair, and because he had a big stomach he looked as if he wasn't wearing anything. Franci giggled and he mistook her laughter for friendliness.

"You kids looking for shells?"

"No," said Lucas, but started looking around because he thought it was a good idea.

The man held up two large shells. "My wife and I come out

early." He pointed to his wife sitting behind him under a beach umbrella. Franci wondered if they had ever been divorced.

"Look at this one, Franci." Lucas lifted one to show her.

"You like that one?" the man asked.

"Yeah. Look!" He held the shell too close for Franci to see and she had to step back. She tried to refuse excitement.

"Well, you can have it," he told Lucas. "Let it be the start of your collection." The wife walked over and in mock harshness asked her husband if he was giving away all the shells again.

"We're just looking at them," Franci told her. "He gave one to Lucas." Franci thought maybe she looked old enough that they expected her to find her own. The man had a large basket full of smaller shells and rocks, and he placed the large conch shells around the basket. Franci wished he would give Lucas one of the big ones.

"My dad isn't here," Lucas said.

"Oh?" said the man.

"He's not dead though," Lucas explained. Once, two weeks ago, when Lucas told a stranger that his dad was gone, the stranger thought he meant he was dead. And by the time Lucas was through explaining, he regretted having mentioned it at all. Sometimes when he said it, he hoped the stranger might tell him what he had done to make it happen.

Franci knew what she had done. On the day her father moved out, just before Franci came home for supper, she and Caroline found two bottles of beer that had been discarded under a bush in Caroline's yard. Each bottle had several sips left in it, so the girls took turns drinking from the bottles and then waited to see if they would feel drunk.

When she came home that night, her mother was in a particular mood and Franci had to pretend that she liked fettuccine. Later, after she and Lucas had cleaned the kitchen and her mother came back from her walk, Franci was sure she had found out about the beer, because her face when she came into the house looked the color of bone meal. And even though Molly told Franci something completely different and never mentioned either the beer or Caroline, still Franci linked this with her father's leaving. Sometimes she wondered what kind of punishment Caroline would get.

The man put some shells in a sack for them, and Franci could see her mother walk toward them. Joe waved and asked if he could go back to the room. He wanted to watch TV and call his father.

He tried several times before he got William. When he did, the secretary answered. She knew Joe's voice.

"Just a minute, Joe. He's here."

"Dad?"

"Everything okay?"

"Yeah. I just wanted to call. Listen," he tried to think of a reason for the call. "Maybe you could call up some of the places where I applied for a job and ask if anything is open yet."

William said he would, and Joe gave him three places to call. Joe had already checked about two of the jobs last week, but he couldn't think of another reason important enough right now, and he had to pretend he was having a good time at the beach. He was becoming adept at these improvisations.

He mentioned that they had been there about an hour and that the water was cold. "We have two rooms," he said.

"Why is that?"

"I don't know."

But before Joe could speak again, William said he had to go, so Joe left the number of his room and told his father to call them tomorrow. When he hung up, the TV seemed unusually loud. He left it that way and watched a late afternoon rerun of "Gilligan's Island."

The first couple of days Molly found Joe brooding in the room and tried to suggest activities that would repudiate his loneliness. Franci and Lucas found friends their own age, and by the third day Joe met a few teenagers who kept asking him to play volleyball. Most of the time Joe refused their offers. He wore his heart like an emblem of defeat.

Molly didn't know how exposed and rowdy Joe felt. How he dreamed of exploring wild lands to build courage against animals ten times his size. How he wished for the challenge of the Himalayas or the Alaskan tundra or rivers in Turkey. He found these thoughts easier than the peculiar schema before him, for which he had no inventory.

"Dad bought a dog," Joe told his mother.

"He did? What kind?"

"A retriever. A golden retriever."

It was the kind of dog William had wanted for many years of their marriage, but Molly always said it would be too much trouble. She wouldn't have it, she said.

"He's already broken out of his pen three times, and he ate Dad's good shoes."

"They can be a lot of trouble," Molly said, vindicated.

"Dad doesn't mind," Joe spoke proudly, and Molly thought he was criticizing her. "His name's Chesapeake. Chess."

She began to defend herself. "Well, if that's the *only* thing you had to look after, it might be all right."

Joe had no idea why she was defending herself. He hadn't accused her in his mind. She straightened up and her gaze flung around the room. She told Joe to come out to the beach with everybody. She said for him to stop feeling sorry for himself.

Wednesday afternoon, one of the teenagers came around to tell Joe about a party at the lifeguard stand. "At eight o'clock," they said.

Molly urged him to move out of the chink he had dug for himself. When she urged him, his body grew like a fortress, and he had the face of an old, sad king. So Molly offered to let him have the car.

It was on that same day that Ben called. He said he wanted to come to the beach for a day or two. Molly welcomed him, though she suggested he stay at another hotel.

Joe heard her talking on the phone. "Was that Dad?"

"No." She told him Ben McGinnis might spend a day or two at the beach.

"I don't think he should do that," Joe said.

"I like him," said Lucas.

"I just don't think it's *right*," Joe urged.

Molly downplayed the immensity of what Joe felt and said it would be fine. "He won't even stay at this hotel."

By eight o'clock a crowd, mostly girls, had gathered at the lifeguard stand. The boys left to get beer. Cokes were kept conspicuously in sight, and a police officer came by once to warn them not to bring beer, but he didn't see anything alcoholic. He said he would be back later.

It was almost ten o'clock before Joe got up enough nerve to speak to Sophie. He had seen her on the beach and spoken to her, but he didn't expect her to be here tonight. She waved to him from where she sat with two other girls. Even though she was sitting, Joe could tell Sophie was taller than the others, but he couldn't tell if she was older or younger than he was.

As he walked to where they sat, he wondered if he looked scruffy. He had shaved this morning but liked to think he needed to shave more often than that. They asked him about people he knew.

Finally one girl said, "You have a car, don't you?" and asked if he had ever gone cow-tipping. Joe said he hadn't, but had heard of it. They were drinking more heavily than he, so he finished his beer and took another one. They had never been cow-tipping either, but John and Norman knew where a place was and how to do it. The place was ten miles out of town. They needed a car.

Joe didn't respond immediately, so Sophie said maybe he would take them out for a burger. She said she was starved, and when Joe agreed they cheered as though someone had won a prize.

Sophie rode next to Joe, her skirt pulled up to her knees and her arm pressed against him. She wore a sleeveless blouse and he could feel how warm her skin was. She asked where he was from. He was sure she was older than he, that she was already in college, but he didn't mention the difference in their ages.

She wore a full white skirt that had huge pockets on the side, and sandals. Her hair was a soft brown and her eyes were what people call robin's-egg blue. Her lips curved nicely and though she didn't talk much, he thought he knew what she was thinking by the way she turned her head or stretched her arms in front of her. Her toenails were painted a bright pink and she wore a yellow blouse. When she moved or touched her hair, she took on the positions of women who pose in shampoo commercials.

They ordered burgers from the window at Hardee's and took the food to a pasture where Norman and John knew the cows stood all night. Norman and John piled into the car and whispered to the other two girls in the back seat. They all seemed to know each other, though not well, and Norman and John brought extra beer. They began to open them in the car.

"Wait till we get there," said one of the girls.

"*You* wait! I'm having mine now!"

"Joe!" said John. "How often you get this car, man?"

"Just tonight."

The girls turned up the radio, and by the time they got to the field everyone had had two beers. Norman took out more.

When they got to a particular road, Joe pulled off to the side.

"Is this *it*?" he asked. They seemed to be nowhere.

"As good as any." Norman took out a joint and lit it. "You ever tried this, man?"

Joe said he had tried it once.

"You want some? A little won't hurt. You can drive with just a little in your head. Besides, we've got the food to bring us down."

They passed the joint around and began to pair off. Sophie stayed with Joe. She asked him if he had ever loved a girl before. Joe said he had, but he didn't know if he had ever been in love. This wasn't quite true, because he was "in love" with Jenny Harrick but didn't know if that counted. Jenny had loved Joe from the seventh through the tenth grade, and in the ninth and tenth grades he loved her back. When she moved to Florida last summer, he visited her for a week and she wrote to him; but he didn't know if that was what people called being in love.

Sophie suggested they walk back into the woods and said she knew where a patch of blackberries grew. She said she loved blackberries, so Joe went with her and they picked some of the berries.

Sophie put them in her pockets, then sat down. She sat as though she were a picture of something.

Joe grew nervous and sweaty. He was afraid she was going to kiss him. She hadn't said anything since she sat down. They could hear the stream nearby.

"Sit down a minute," Sophie said and made a sound almost like a laugh. He hoped she didn't think he was stupid.

Sophie pulled his head to her shoulder and let him rest there, though he hadn't asked to rest. He hadn't asked for anything. He tried to think of something to say that wouldn't sound foolish. She began to kiss him.

Then suddenly there was nothing but Sophie and her skirt pulled above her waist and Joe with his hand on the inside of her leg, high, where she let his fingers push against her. She pushed back, then touched him, not as though she knew how to touch, just as if she were finding out something herself.

Then she said, "Please," and again, "Please," because she was afraid he might not want to do this. But nothing could have been further from Joe's mind, because she removed her blouse and didn't wear a bra, and because her breast touched his face like a soft bud, and she kept saying please, please.

Joe couldn't imagine how she would remember this, or if he would see her again. His head began to swim and the drunken mix of beer and pot took effect. He felt the beginnings of nausea, but wasn't aware of it yet because Sophie whispered to him, and he went inside her, pushing past the place that hurt her. He was surprised, because he was sure Sophie had done this, but she hadn't. He could feel blood rush onto her skirt and the blackberries crush in her pockets. He could smell the blood odor.

Joe didn't last long inside her, but in a few moments, even before he came out, he grew large again. And this time he stayed longer, until Sophie made a sound that he felt sure was pleasure.

He lay beside her in the grass, her blouse still off and the stains on her skirt, which they would try to wash out in the stream. They could hear the others running toward the cows, trying to knock over one sleepy beast, make her fall. It seemed to Joe a cruel thing to do. Then he told Sophie he loved her. He said it because he wanted now to love someone, and wanted it to be this girl. He thought if he loved her that his life might change.

They went to the stream to wash Sophie off and she wrapped the arms of a sweater around her waist to cover the stains. As they went to the car, they called for the others to come, and Joe wondered how he might think back on this moment when he got old, if he would see it as love. He imagined he would, but he wondered if Sophie would look back on it the same way.

He was beginning to feel very sick but couldn't trust anyone else to drive. The ten miles home seemed like fifty, but when he drove into the hotel parking lot, he tried to make himself presentable.

Molly heard Joe unlock the door. "Is that you, Joe?" She heard the few moments it took for him to hook the chain. "You okay?"

"Yeah."

Lucas and Franci lay asleep and Joe stepped out of his clothes, but knocked something off the dresser as he fell against it. Lucas and Franci didn't wake up, but Molly came into their room.

"What's the matter?"

Joe didn't answer. He hoped she wouldn't follow him into the bathroom, but as he stepped under the fluorescent lighting, his face had such a wheaten pallor that Molly asked if he felt sick.

"Just tired." Joe felt an attack of nausea coming on and couldn't hold it back. He vomited into the sink.

"You're drunk," Molly accused. She could smell him. "How much have you had?" She didn't want to know, only to accuse.

Joe didn't hear, because he was leaning into the sink. She told him—and he did hear this—that she would call his father the next day. The way she yelled, it seemed directed more at William than at him. She left the bathroom, telling him to clean everything up, that she didn't want to look at him.

Joe sat on the floor. Vomit spread from the sink to the toilet. He couldn't feel sorry. He wished he had the courage to do something rash. Nothing he did was rash enough. He wanted to see Sophie again.

He cleaned out the sink and used all the towels, even the towel Franci was saving—for what, he didn't know. He vomited once more, then went to bed.

Lucas heard everything. He usually slept with Joe, but when he heard Joe getting sick, he moved to Franci's bed. Joe was glad to find his bed empty.

"Did you get sick?" Lucas asked in a dark, whispery voice. He wanted to say something, anything.

"Yes."

The next morning Joe heard his mother call William's apartment. No one answered, so she tried the office. He was supposed to call back. It was nearly ten-thirty and Molly still hadn't said anything to Joe about last night, though she checked to see how he felt and brought him hot tea and toast. When she finally sat on his bed, he didn't pretend to be asleep.

"Did you get hold of Dad?" He did pretend he hadn't heard her call him.

Molly looked as though she wanted to say something but that it had been memorized and she couldn't think of how it started. She spoke calmly and deliberately. She said he would be grounded when they got home.

"Why did you drink so much?" she asked.

"I didn't know I was. It sneaked up on me."

"Did you smoke anything?" Joe could tell she didn't know how to ask this. "Did you do any drugs?" This is what she worried about.

"No." He needed to lie about this. "It was just beer."

He couldn't tell if she believed him or just chose to believe him for the moment.

It was noon before he got up and put on his clothes. He could hear Lucas and Franci in his mother's room playing gin rummy. He slipped back on the pants he'd worn last night and went in to be with them. He hoped he didn't smell too strongly of Sophie.

"Where'd you get the money?" he asked. They played with real money.

"Mama gave us four dollars in quarters and dimes." Franci showed Joe her hand. Her pile of change was growing low and she wanted to quit before she lost everything to Lucas. But Lucas wanted to keep playing on the chance he might win more.

"You just spend it as fast as you get it," Franci said. She was right. Lucas liked to have money but didn't care about the money itself. Franci cared about the money, while Lucas cared about the pleasure.

"*He who wishes to become rich in a day is hanged in a year*," Franci said.

"Deal me in," said Joe. He reached into his pants pocket to add his own money to the pile. But Joe hadn't been sitting with them for long before Lucas said, "I smell something funny," and scrunched his nose toward Joe. "What do I *smell*?"

CHAPTER
EIGHT

William could not even think of them at the beach without him. He went to the house once, because he needed to get the rest of his clothes. He and Molly had decided he should do this while everyone was gone. It took him three hours, but before he placed the key back in its hiding place, he sat down in the den, just to see what it felt like to be in the house alone. The house felt different to him, and he couldn't think about the rest of his life.

From the house he made a call to the beach. "I wanted to tell you I've finished moving things out," he said. He sat in his usual chair. "It's all out. The things we talked about."

As he spoke, Molly sank down. She didn't know what to say. "Well, good."

"How's the beach?"

"Fine." He hadn't received the message yet about Joe. "Will, I don't know what to do about Joe."

"What's the matter?" And she told him all that had happened, all that she knew about.

"I'll handle it," he said. He sounded firm and in control. "Tell him

I'll call tonight. Then when you get home, we'll decide how to ground him for a while. Tell him that."

When Molly went back to the beach, she took her sketch pad and drew a long, thin ensemble of clouds formed like an archipelago on the horizon. She drew the pale broken line of the beach, and she wanted to ask someone, anyone walking by: What is going on?

But the natural arrangement around her—the line of the horizon, the moving line of shore, and far off the rumor of clouds—this placement created a meaning. The line and color heightened her insight, and to sketch this on her pad touched something in her like a hymn.

William went back to his office, where he found a note from his secretary saying there was trouble with Joe and to call this number. He stared at the number, but he couldn't get out of his mind the smell of the house, or of Molly, so he placed his hands on his big, dumb knees and tried to hoist this mood from his head.

Ben arrived the next day and took everyone out to dinner. He didn't stay at their hotel but close by. He took them to a place they named as their favorite, but conversation was awkward. No one but Molly wanted Ben to be there. Joe didn't say three words during the whole meal but held his mouth in a benign smile. Ben suggested they play miniature golf, and Lucas and Franci leapt at the proposition. Joe didn't object because he was already in so much trouble.

Everyone picked a different-colored ball and Molly suggested they choose up teams to make it more exciting. She said she and Franci were the captains and would pick sides. Molly chose Joe first. Franci picked Ben for the practical reason that she might win if she picked him and because she felt sorry for him. She thought he was trying hard. Lucas said he wanted to be on Franci's side, but no one knew why he chose to say that.

They played the best two out of three games. Molly and Joe won the first, Franci's team the second, and the third game was a close race until the last hole, when Joe made a hole in one and was proclaimed the night's champion. Joe knew the experience of being a champion. At eight years old he had hit a home run and won the game for his team. At ten he did it again and they carried him off the field on their shoulders.

The manager gave Joe the free pass that comes with a hole in one, and Joe asked if he could have two more, for his brother and sister.

Back at the hotel, Ben said goodnight to everyone. He thanked them for letting him be part of their vacation, and for a moment he got almost too serious in the way he thanked them, so he made a joke about himself and everyone laughed it off. He told Molly he would see her on the beach tomorrow.

The next day was cloudy, and Ben found Molly sketching under an umbrella. He read to her from a book he'd brought. Molly liked the sound of his voice reading to her and she kept sketching. Without using any color, she gave the beach a rough texture and made the sky into evening by shading it like a bruise. She thought of giving one of the sketches to Zack and wondered which one he would like.

On the last day it rained. Ben left early that morning, and since it was raining Joe and Franci were ready to leave too. Lucas wanted to stay, in case it cleared up.

Joe rode in the front seat, but didn't ask to drive. Rain lashed against the window and the wiper's dull blades left streaks of water that were never smoothed off.

"Mom," Franci said, "why'd you name me Franci?" She pronounced Fran-ci with a slow lilt, the way kids at school said it to tease her.

"After Papa Frank. You know that."

"You gave us bad names, Mom," said Lucas. "Except for Joe. His name's all right."

"Well, I used to hate my name too," she told them. But her experience was irrelevant to what they thought they were saying.

Franci sat up and leaned over the front seat. "When it's my birthday again, I'm going to change it to Rosa." Then she reminded them that her birthday was on Friday.

"I know," said Molly, but in fact she had forgotten that Franci's birthday came so soon after they got home. "Have you thought about who you'll ask to your party?" Molly gave a party every year, to every child, so they expected it.

"I've already asked people." Franci counted on her fingers, naming the guests. "Ten," she said. "No, eleven counting me."

"No boys?" Joe asked. He had listened for boys' names.

"It's a slumber party."

Molly told her that was too many to ask to spend the night.

"Some of them won't be able to come," Franci promised.

"I already got her something." Lucas spoke from his corner in the back seat.

"Tell me what it is." Molly turned her ear to him, and Lucas leaned forward to whisper his present.

"I *heard* that," said Joe. "You whisper so *loud.*"

"I do not. What'd I say?"

Joe whispered to Lucas what Lucas had whispered to his mother, and Lucas said, "That's not it! That's not it at all. You are *way* off!"

Joe didn't argue, but made a laughing noise through his nose. Franci told them she wanted a radio Walkman, a sweatshirt with Genesis on the front (which is what Lucas had whispered), a curling iron (which they told her probably wouldn't work, because her hair was so thin and straight), and some eye makeup. She didn't know what kind.

"Eye makeup?" Lucas scooted back into his corner and felt betrayed—his secret was known by everyone and now Franci wanted eye makeup. "That's stupid. Why do you want that?"

"You would look ri*dic*ulous," Joe told her.

"Listen, honey," said Molly, "your eyes are so lovely you probably won't ever need to use eye makeup. That's for people who don't have eyes like yours."

The birthday party turned out to be twelve girls, because one brought a friend from out of town. All arrived with sleeping bags, pillows, huge radios, tapes, hot hair curlers, water balloons, and cans of shaving cream to spray in case anyone fell asleep.

Early that morning Molly got up with the determination to do everything right and to bake an unforgettable cake. She used separate ingredients rather than a mix. She measured flour, sugar, butter—real butter, and melted blocks of bitter chocolate. Franci came downstairs to make sure the cake smell was for her. She worked with her mother, deciding to make two cakes instead of one, and to make one three layers tall. As they worked, Molly's mind opened, came loose like a fist opening. She hadn't known it had been held so tight.

Lucas licked bowls all day—whatever batter or frosting they made, he asked to lick the bowl and spatulas, so Molly would say, "Why, I won't even have to wash this, you've made it so clean." He wanted her to say that every time.

When the girls arrived, Lucas kept going in and out of the room where they rolled out their sleeping bags. The girls spread themselves all through the downstairs and didn't seem to mind if they weren't completely dressed when Lucas came in. Lucas acted as though he didn't notice their nakedness, and he hung around. He saw them put on their pajamas.

They hadn't used the water balloons, but filled a few with water and threatened each other. Lucas found a balloon, filled it quietly, and tied it closed. Then at a particular moment he threw it at the girl with the flimsiest shorty pajamas. He watched to see what she would do.

The balloon proved to be stronger than it looked and wasn't filled up enough to break. It dropped heavily on the floor next to the girl, and the others laughed at the fact that it didn't break and at the funny way it bounced. Lucas thought they laughed at him, and he tried to smile. He picked up the balloon and ran outside. He threw it against a tree, hard, and broke the thick skin. Water burst out.

"You should've seen it!" he told the girls when he went back in. He was yelling. It was important for them to know what he had done.

But they didn't care. "Where is your brother?" they asked Franci, ignoring Lucas. They wanted to see Joe.

"He's around somewhere." So they kept looking for Joe to show up, to poke his head in and make them scream. Lucas went upstairs, but first he announced to everyone he was going to look for Joe. When he came up the stairs, he found his mother instead.

"What's going on down there?"

"Nothing." He climbed onto the bed beside her. "It's *boring*."

Molly watched "Hill Street Blues," or had it on. She mended one of Joe's shirts. "You need anything mended while I have this out?"

"Naw." They watched more of "Hill Street" until a commercial came on, then Lucas performed the trick of cupping his hand beneath his right armpit and bringing the arm down fast enough to make a graphic scatological sound.

"Lucas!"

He did it two more times. "You know what that sounds like?" he asked her.

"I *know*." Molly put down her mending and tried cupping her own hand, but couldn't bring her arm down fast enough to make anything but a faint slapping sound. Lucas instructed her several times, but she couldn't do it.

"You're good!" she told him. "Who taught you that?"

"Joe did." Then he said, "Did Joe go out?"

"He wasn't supposed to." Molly looked at the clock. "Is his car gone?" She bit off the end of the thread and stuck the needle into the small upholstered tomato. "He was supposed to tell me if he was going to your dad's. Are you sure he isn't in his room?"

They both went to Joe's room. The phone lay on the floor and clothes were strewn everywhere. Some towels and shirts, still dirty from the beach, made his room smell like fish.

"He was supposed to finish washing these clothes," Molly told Lucas, and she picked up a few of the worst pieces and threw them into the hall. "This stuff's been here for two days." She found a wet towel laid across his bed. "I *told* him."

"He's probably over at Dad's."

Molly called William.

"How's the birthday party?" William asked.

"Okay. The real stuff doesn't get started until later though."

"I remember."

"Did Joe come over there?"

"He called and said he might come. I discouraged him. He went to Andrew's house, I think."

"I mean, did he plan to stay with you tonight?"

"He didn't say."

"I usually find out a little more than that, Will."

"He's all right. I told him he had to be in early. I talked to him, Molly."

"He's supposed to be *grounded*."

"I thought that started tomorrow. That's what we told him. After Franci's party."

"I'll leave the key outside."

"You worry too much, Molly. He's just growing up. You've got to let go."

She knew that. "I know that," she said. "I'm just tired of hearing it."

"You're just tired of hearing me tell you."

She felt dismissed and thought William sounded unshakably poised. "You have somebody there?" she asked, as though after all these years she had a right to know.

"Yes," he said, and gave her that right.

"I'm sorry." But what Molly was sorry about was the configuration of Franci's thirteenth birthday, William's apartment, and Joe's wide wall. It was a strange backwash of sorriness composed for this moment.

"Mom!" Franci yelled from downstairs. Her voice was high and desperate. "Come get Lucas! He's being mean."

"Lucas! Come upstairs now."

"He's not coming!"

"Lucas!"

She tucked Lucas into bed. She didn't want to read to him, but he felt left out of Franci's party. Franci treated him differently when her friends were around. So Molly read from an ongoing mystery story they took turns reading each night.

"One more," he said.

"No."

"One."

"It's late, Lucas. I'm tired."

But Lucas pulled out *Where the Wild Things Are* by Maurice Sendak. Molly could always be counted on to read that book.

"All the wild things are downstairs," she told Lucas, and they nudged each other in a way that made them feel superior and intimate.

It was eleven-thirty before Molly got into bed, and at eleven forty-five the doorbell rang. She heard the girls scramble to see who it was. They thought someone had come to see them. Molly closed the door to the den to shut out the noise.

A man stood before her. He had on a uniform and when he spoke his voice was rigid and thick. "Mrs. Hanner?" he said. "I am Sergeant Gold."

And Molly thought her life was over.

What the sergeant told her was that Joe had been in a car wreck with two other boys. The car went off a bridge and into the French Broad River. The flooding from the last few weeks made the water so dangerous that the sergeant gave Molly no hope of finding the boys alive. They'd found one of the bodies, he told her, and were dragging the river for the other two.

Molly had only barely let the sergeant into the house. She could hear the girls laughing in the other room. The light on the backyard was from a full moon and she could see how long the grass was. Joe had mown the yard a week ago. The sergeant named the other two boys, but Molly couldn't remember what Roy Mathis looked like. She knew Andrew—his mischief, his unruly manners. "Miz Hanner, mind if I stay for dinner? Miz Hanner, did you burn the brownies again?"

"We found your son's jacket," the sergeant said. He knew that at times like this it was best if you didn't say the name of the son except in a very formal way. "And we found a portion of the wallet belonging to Andrew Hawkins."

The sergeant said it looked as though the brakes had failed and also that they were going down that stretch of mountain a little fast. No one mentioned drinking, and Molly hoped no one would ever mention it. It was too late for blame.

"My husband doesn't live here," Molly told him. "Does he know?"

"You're the first one I've talked to," the sergeant said.

Molly was the first to know. "I'll call him," she said. "Now could you tell me again exactly what happened?" and her mind took it down as a reporter would for an article. When the sergeant said it again, it was as though she heard it for the first time, and she interrupted him (though it was just a whisper), "Wait, wait." If Sergeant Gold could just wait, not say it, it wouldn't be true. When she went to the phone to dial William's number, she couldn't remember it and had to call information to have it told to her.

"If they haven't found him yet," William said, "then how do they know it was Joe? It wasn't Joe's car, was it?"

"No. It was Andrew's car. Andrew was driving, I think."

"Maybe Joe wasn't with them, Molly. He likes to drive his own car, you know. And they say that Joe's car is still at Andrew's house?"

"Yes."

"Maybe he wasn't with them, Molly."

"Will. We have to go down to the police station." The sergeant stood beside her looking out the window as though he couldn't hear a word she said. Franci and her friends were chasing the grey cat.

"But they're not sure."

"We have to go down there. Will, I'm not going to tell Franci anything yet."

"God, Molly, I don't know what to do."

"Come pick me up."

William said he would.

The sergeant went ahead of them downtown, where he would

have to tell them again of the accident. He had had experience in the number of times he needed to repeat an incident like this so that the realization could finally take hold. The first time he told it, each word entered the air and people heard only bits and pieces which they said back to him, and the sergeant filled in all the parts that were missed, until it came down on them altogether.

"Mr. Hanner?" The sergeant led them to a small room and closed the door. "Your wife has told you?" And he proceeded to say it again, with Molly listening as though she hadn't heard it two times before.

Joe had been playing cards at Andrew Hawkins' house, but he left with Andrew and Roy Mathis to get some food. That was about eleven o'clock, according to the other boys in the house. They were drinking beer, but nothing stronger, and the boys said Joe hadn't had any. They said Andrew drank more than the others.

William asked which boy had been found, and the sergeant told him Andrew Hawkins. "Should we go to where they're dragging the river? Should we go out there?" William turned to direct his question to Molly, but the sergeant answered.

"No sir, I don't think you should do that. You go back home. We'll call you when we find him."

William took Molly home, and when she got out of the car he said, "We should've brought something back with us. His clothes, or something. I thought we were going to get his jacket."

"We'll get that," Molly said. Their words were hidden outside the realm of anything real. They couldn't measure their resistance to what had happened, but felt, both of them, beyond the reach of thought. William walked her to the door but didn't want to leave. He lingered the way a young boy lingers expecting to kiss his girl good-night.

"You want to come in?"

He did. He wanted to see Lucas and Franci. He had to make sure they were present and intact.

The den was full of girls, and Lucas lay asleep with his legs hung over the side of a chair. A sheet was draped partially over him.

"Mrs. Hanner." One girl with huge rollers in her hair explained Lucas' presence. "He woke up and wanted to sleep down here."

"That's okay." Molly lifted Lucas to carry him upstairs, but William took him from her.

"Where'd you and Daddy go?" Franci asked. It seemed odd for them to be carrying Lucas upstairs together. In a way it seemed odd, and in a way it seemed like what they had always done but weren't doing anymore.

Molly shook her head to decline an answer. "It's time you girls got quiet," she said.

William carried Lucas to bed and Molly opened a window to let in fresh air. A baseball cap and a few toys lay on his bed. Molly picked some of his clothes off the floor.

"You can stay here tonight," Molly offered. Her voice sounded hollow, even to herself.

"No," William said, then "No," and the second time sounded more sure. "I'll be here tomorrow. Early.'" He leaned toward Lucas. "Should I wake him up?"

Molly knew how he felt. "You'll be here tomorrow. Let's wait to tell them then."

William held her in the darkness of the room, and they cried without believing what they cried about. As they went downstairs and out to the car each had a delicate concern for the other, and for a moment Molly thought he might change his mind about staying, but he got into his car.

"What will we do?" he asked Molly.

Molly didn't know, but she didn't say she didn't know.

Before going to her room, where she was sure she would not sleep, maybe never sleep again, she told the girls to keep everything quiet, and she went to check once more on Lucas. He had already kicked off the covers, and she pulled them back over him. Then she leaned to kiss his forehead, and though she had never done so before, she put her head to his chest and listened for his heartbeat.

In the hallway lay Joe's wet clothes and a towel. Molly threw them into his room, but before she closed his door, she stepped in. He was alive in here at least. The unmade bed, sheets with a geometric pattern, posters on the wall, pennants. The phone cord stretched across the room to the bed, and Molly felt delirious to look at it. She picked up a toothbrush and razor, and realized she didn't know how often Joe shaved. She tried not to fix her mind on thoughts of the future or let any impression of despair kindle her heart. The edge of her mind felt precarious with the flickering knowledge that nothing would ever be the same.

She lifted a pair of Joe's shorts and a shirt. She smelled them to test their dirtiness, but when she did this, touched his clothes and smelled the strong extract of his body, the sight of him came with the smell and her memory could not stop its folly.

He will come in later, she thought.

And the thread that had held her through all the sergeant's telling, and the disbelief in William's questions, came loose—her face unraveled and her arms. And when the snap came she reached down to pick up the phone, thinking she must straighten things a little, still thinking that order could help. But the long cord swept like one blind arm across the desk, knocking down Joe's collection of arrowheads. His trophies and desk lamp fell everywhere.

There was a sound that came from Molly's throat—loud, though not loud enough. And when she turned around, she faced his closet. She didn't mean to but reached in and put her arms around all his clothes. She pulled them out, but the bar came out with them and she fell backwards onto the floor. When she looked up, she saw all the girls and Lucas standing in the doorway.

"Mama?" Franci's voice restored Molly to her position in the room.

"Fran-ci." She said the name Franci hated. "Come here." She motioned for Lucas to come too, and tried to imagine what must be in their minds.

The girls scattered downstairs as though this were a joke that had been played on them, but they hadn't understood it yet. Molly followed to explain how something had happened and it might be better if they all went to sleep. In the morning they could have doughnuts and orange juice and call their mothers to come get them. She said Franci would not be back downstairs.

"Joe was in a car wreck," Molly told them. Franci and Lucas had one face when she said it. "He and Andrew and Roy drove down a mountain. They went off a bridge into the river." Lucas began to cry and Molly pulled him under her arm. "They're looking for him now."

"Is that why Daddy was here?"

"Yes. He'll be here tomorrow. He'll talk to you about it then. But now I want us to sleep, all of us, in my bed."

Franci started to cry when her mother said this, this part seeming final to her—sleeping together. They undressed, and Lucas and Franci positioned themselves on either side of their mother, settling into a delicate balance as though they were sick.

Molly turned out the light. She felt woozy with grief. The only sound was the noise of cars passing on the road, making light go all around the room. When the children were little, Molly used to play a game with the shadows made by cars. She wanted to ask them if they had forgotten the game. She hoped they had not forgotten anything.

Molly lay for thirty minutes, listening for the breathing of their sleep. Her eyes stung with dryness and she couldn't be still. She kept thinking of the time Joe was carried off the field on the shoulders of his teammates. She saw so clearly his face from that day and she got up to go to his room.

Moonlight came in and made the room itself look astonished. His clothes lay scattered in postures of surprise. Molly sat down. She wanted to sleep under his clothes. She made a pillow of his shirts and pulled his clothes over her, feeling the tribute of heavy jeans and the pleasure of T-shirts. Whatever she touched came alive in her hand.

And as she lay there she could breathe him in—the sour sweaty smell of his head when he was little and played in the yard, the boy-smell of dust and hot soot. And she slept in that smell, so that when she dozed off at about five-thirty, he seemed alive to her then.

CHAPTER
NINE

William was there by eight o'clock the next morning. Joe's car sat in the driveway. Someone had brought it over for them, but when William saw it in the driveway he believed for a moment that the previous night was a mistake and Joe was home now. The moment penetrated him with so much relief that when the knowledge set back in, he had already believed the other was true, and it all came back with an interior flicker that had the weight of tons.

Joe's car keys lay on the front seat, his jacket on the floor in the back. The jacket was muddy and wet. William sat down behind the wheel, his movements so slow that someone watching him would think he was sneaking away. A history book lay on the seat beside him and there was a note indicating that Joe owed four dollars for late charges. The book opened naturally to a chapter about Indians, and the pages in that section were underlined and dog-eared. William put the keys in the ignition to hear the radio station Joe would have listened to. He heard the end of a rock song.

The mother of one of the girls from Franci's party drove up while William was in the car. He didn't hear her drive up or leave. He entered the kitchen and called to Molly, or anyone. Orange juice glasses and doughnuts were on the counter beside the sink. He called again and heard no answer, so went upstairs to find them asleep in Joe's room. The room in the morning light appeared scandalous.

William whispered so he wouldn't wake Lucas and Franci. They were covered with sweatshirts and jeans, and William picked up a sock from Molly's arm. "Did you sleep at all?"

"A little, I think." Lucas' arm was thrown across her chest and Molly lifted it off. "Did you?"

"No."

William had brought the paper and he held it up to show Molly he had it. "There's a write-up in here," he said, and Molly put on a robe to go downstairs. She asked if he wanted some breakfast.

Before they got downstairs, William told Molly that Joe's car was in the driveway. "Somebody brought it over from Andrew's house." Molly nodded and took out eggs and bacon and two blueberry muffins she had been saving. William began to fill the dishwasher with glasses and bowls. Every time he leaned over, Molly could see the dry slope of his head and his pitiful composure.

As she scrambled eggs and cooked a pan of bacon, William read her the article, which he had already read to himself.

THREE PRESUMED DEAD AS CAR VEERS OFF BRIDGE

Andrew Hawkins was killed Friday night when a car with two other passengers veered off the Oconee Bridge into the French Broad River. Roy Mathis and Joseph Hanner are still missing.

At ten forty-five p.m. Sergeant Barry Gold received a call describing an accident reported by a couple driving along the Oconee Bridge Road. Mr. and Mrs. Jack Harrison told the sergeant that the car "seemed to lose control." Mrs. Harrison said "about halfway down the hill it looked like they lost control of their brakes." The roads were slippery from the recent rains and the car presumably skidded through the siderail and off the bridge. The French Broad River has been at its highest level for weeks.

Many volunteers have joined the search. The body of Andrew Hawkins was found wedged in the driver's seat of the car.

William read only part of the article to Molly. He didn't read the part that described a group of boys telling how Andrew and Roy and Joe went out to get pizza and when they didn't come back in an hour the boys heard sirens and went to see what had happened. "We never really thought anything had happened to them though," one boy said. "I still can't believe it."

The morning was quiet except for the birds, and a dog barking. It was Saturday and people slept late. Molly stayed in her robe, and to see her like this seemed to Will more than a familiar sight. It seemed a refuge, like a beloved doll. She set the table and put down a large platter of scrambled eggs and bacon, some strawberries she had hidden from the slumber-party girls, and two blueberry muffins.

As soon as William stopped reading, Molly knew he had begun to blame himself. "Now, Will." She spoke with the emphasis of someone who knew better. William didn't look up, and though Molly couldn't hear his words exactly, she knew he regretted not letting Joe stay with him last night.

"Even if you'd let him stay, he would've gone for a while to Andrew's house." William tried to believe her. Molly poured more coffee, and the bare memory of what their life was seemed now like the trace of a song.

"Lucas." Franci woke and heard her mother and father downstairs.

"What!"

"Listen!"

"What?"

"They're downstairs."

"So?" Lucas pulled Joe's shirt up to his neck as if it were a sheet. "What are we supposed to do?" he asked her.

She had no idea.

The evening paper had another write-up two columns long, and Molly cut it out. An obituary and front-page article on Andrew made her fold the paper and keep it all, because she couldn't undertake the distinct activity of cutting any more. The paper announced a memorial service for all three boys on Wednesday.

Jill came to the house before they had finished breakfast. She came in the door and went straight to Molly. She held her, then went to William and held him too. As they spoke to Jill they spoke, both William and Molly, as though it were a matter of time before Joe would be found. He would be in bad shape, but alive. Jill listened, but felt insensible.

People came by the house with cakes and casseroles. Jill took charge, and Molly got dressed. William sat in the den and didn't move for long periods of time. He liked being in the house where noises kept his mind at bay, but he caught himself looking for Joe. He kept thinking of things he'd forgotten to tell him.

Ben came by, but he called first. He stayed for a short time and tried to talk to Molly, but he couldn't say what he wished. He left, promising to call her later.

Franci and Lucas wandered the house as if it were no longer their own. Molly suggested they watch TV. The den had people sitting around, but no one objected when Franci turned on the TV. No one objected to anything they did.

"What do you want to watch?" Franci asked Lucas.

"I don't know." Franci didn't usually give him a choice. "Maybe there's a movie." They wanted to watch something long.

The proximity of others' conversations and the mention of Joe and Roy and Andrew made the distractions unyielding. Lucas sat Indian fashion, close enough so his knees touched Franci. In a few minutes Franci said, "I'll be back in a little while," and got up. Lucas didn't ask where she was going.

Joe's bed had a different bedspread and Franci didn't know when her mother had done this. The clothes were hung up and all his trophies and his shoebox of arrowheads were arranged neatly on his desk. All the same pennants were on the wall. She didn't know why she expected them to be gone. Last year Franci had begged Joe for the Wake Forest pennant, but Joe refused and told her to buy one for herself. He hated telling her no.

"They don't make that one anymore," Franci argued. She thought of taking it now, but hated herself. She didn't want it as much as she did last year but thought of it anyway.

William came upstairs and sat beside Franci on the bed. "What're you doing?"

"Nothing."

"You might want to take something from in here," he said.

"Yeah, maybe." She went over to Joe's shelf, pretending to care about something other than the pennant.

William's eyes memorized the room. "We'll probably leave it as it is for a while." He couldn't judge how it should be changed, and Franci could tell by what he said that he thought Joe was dead. When they went out, William closed the door. He hoped no one else would go in there. It spoiled something to see anyone there.

In William's head there was nothing but the wild crack of hard ground. If only he could eat stones and bring Joe back, if he could just find the sharp feathers to put together a partial wing for his soul. He was afraid that when he sat at his apartment without Joe his silence would have no accompaniment. Molly sat on the porch. She motioned for Will to join her. Neither of them spoke. They sat under the night sky and looked toward the shoulder of a hill.

Louise and Sig came the next day and picked up Molly's father at the airport. When Frank Bates got off the plane, he had the expression of someone drugged, and Louise and Sig found it difficult to engage him in any kind of conversation at all. They did not tell this to Molly.

People came to the house for days. Zack came too. He lived at the farm with Louise and Sig most of the time now, but he came back when he heard about Joe.

Molly saw Zack standing outside in the yard. She was about to go to the side door and call him in when she saw him take large heel-hitting strides up the front steps. The door was already open, so he came in, unnoticed until someone said, "Molly, Zack is here."

He stood before Molly without speaking at first, then he said simply, "I heard about Joe." His arm flew out, distracted. "I wanted to come by."

Molly walked with him to the table of food. She prepared a plate, asking what he wanted. Zack nodded to everything. She went with him to the corner of the den. He ate slowly and without hunger. Lucas spoke to him, and George Kirby made an attempt to be polite. Others welcomed Zack but didn't know what to say to him. They accepted now the permanence of his manners. But the way he sat so still made everyone feel he could read their minds.

After a few minutes he put his plate into the sink, rinsing it off, then stepped out the side door. He did not speak to William.

The memorial service for all three boys was a long one, because the young people were allowed to speak. The minister spoke last. He made comments directly to the parents in a way that was both public and private. He ended with a prayer for the safe discovery of the other two boys, but he asked too for the courage to bear what had happened.

The service was at the graveside, and when Andrew's casket was lowered Molly drew in a breath and put her hand on Lucas' shoulder. She could see Ben's sweet face in the crowd, and she kept her eyes on him. But in that moment when Andrew was lowered, Molly had to remember that this was *not* Joe, and the view of her life sat raw before her. And though she had never experienced it before, she stood without any idea of a future at all.

Their days went by in an unnumbered haze and finally it was a week with no sign of Roy or Joe. William was back in his apartment, though he called Molly every day. Jill came by most nights to eat supper with them, and Frank Bates stayed to cook all the meals. He slept on the sofa bed in Molly's studio, and she liked his presence in the house. She especially liked the stale, flameless odor of him in the morning, and his voice speaking to Lucas and Franci at the table.

Lucas and Franci devoted themselves to each other and to the fox. They ran to the creek in the mornings and built dams or swam at the waterfall. But there were other days when no one spoke much in the house or days when Ben came over. They could not remember how to be polite.

Molly didn't wash her hair, but let it hang stringy around her shoulders. She sat on the porch most days without getting dressed, and in the evening she concentrated on the inexhaustible energy of moths landing on the various surfaces around her. She wanted to study their ecstatic, short lives.

Ben took her for long drives. She rode with him, but nothing much was talked about. She talked with William often, but didn't mention her lethargy.

"They found Roy. They found Roy!" Franci yelled the news across the yard. It had been two weeks. "They found him down at the quarry."

"Oh, Franci." The way Franci said it, it seemed something they should rejoice about—not because the body was found, but because it wasn't Joe. And though Franci was glad it wasn't Joe, Molly wished every day for the ritual of seeing Joe's body, because until she saw it she could not stop hoping. Each day she waited for the final impact, and that impact came again and again.

"Maybe they'll find Joe soon," she said, because she couldn't stand, literally could not stand, the thought of not finding him at all. She went in to call Roy's mother.

Mrs. Mathis was divorced and had three older children. Roy was younger by ten years than the others. He was the child of her old age. Molly tried again to picture how he looked, but couldn't. She could not believe, though she had heard this as truth, that after a few years she would have trouble recalling the details of Joe's face.

Yesterday Jill took Molly downtown, and a boy who looked like Joe ran across the street about half a block in front of them. He had Joe's jerky stride, and when Molly saw it a short gasp escaped from her throat, coming quietly from her mouth in the shape of an O. Jill pulled to a side street and parked the car for a few moments.

"I thought it was Joe," Molly said.

"I know."

"I mean I really thought it was him." She struggled to take a Kleenex from her purse. She carried Kleenex all the time now. She felt trapped in a light from the past—memory that could trap her and suck her down a black hole. *When a star loses its envelope and becomes, what does it become, when the envelope is sucked off by a black hole's pull? It's*

*like closing the door to the springhouse one night when I stepped inside and
fastened it shut—no crack of light, but my allegiance pledges to see it, if it
comes.* She imagined herself trying to stand in deep water.

The next day the newspaper prominently displayed a picture of
Roy Mathis, and Louise called to say she would visit Molly on Saturday. She would come by herself.

It was Thursday when William called during the middle of the
night. He asked Molly to come over. It had been two and a half
weeks. He said he was afraid he couldn't move his legs, that he felt
paralyzed. Molly didn't get dressed, but put on a robe and drove to
William's apartment.

She had been inside his apartment twice, and both times were
nights she brought Franci and Lucas to stay with him. Once she
walked in and William asked her advice about some plants. He even
made coffee, and they drank it while Franci and Lucas watched TV.
For a short time on those two nights the assembly of them there felt
normal.

William couldn't move his legs, and he showed Molly how he'd
been trying to get up and walk. His legs collapsed whenever he
stood up, and he pulled himself onto the bed.

"Did you ever have this before?"

He tried to remember. "Once. When my father died."

"Will."

"Molly, you're the only one who misses Joe the way I do. I mean,
nobody knows how this feels but you."

They made love that night, because what they loved was the
shared hope that Joe would be found, or even be alive. They talked
of ways it could be true.

Their hearts felt like stones, but while William was inside her,
they both believed from some hard core that Joe was alive. When
they believed it together, they had the fine company of stones, and
slept for hours in each other's arms. They made love again before
Molly went home, but after that night neither of them spoke of what
they had done.

Molly entered her house before it was light. She watched the sun come up, seeing the curious light begin and burn itself soft. She liked to see how the light changed, to be awake when the crazy sun struck over the trees, to hear birds cradled in the slow wash of it.

But this morning, even after being with William, and all during the day, Molly thought of Ben. She thought of the way he said her name. She thought of the sweet chain his smile built between them, and how she didn't want one link of that chain to be broken.

"How did you know where I was?" Molly asked Louise.

"Franci said you might need a ride home."

Molly taught a class at the Arts Council on Saturdays. She said she was almost ready to leave. Louise scanned the students' work. One sketch was of a child in bed, the posture languorous, but the child held something tightly in his hand. No other figures intruded, except for a dog in the corner. The dog was awake. There was a depth and proximity in the figures and also in the doorway which looked into a farther room.

On the way home Louise commented on that sketch and let their conversation stay on the surface, but Molly dove beneath the surface when she said, "Louise?" It was a question Molly had wondered about, but hadn't asked. "Why haven't you and Sig ever adopted a child?" It sounded accusatory, but Louise never took remarks as accusations, even if they were meant that way.

"It was something we thought about." Her expression was desultory, and she stopped before she said the next thing. They had reached Molly's house and Louise wanted to see if they would go in or finish the conversation in the car.

"Years ago," she blurted out, not like confiding, but more like releasing it, "we had a son. We had him until one week before he was fourteen." Molly didn't move her hands from the wheel. She felt she should move, but her hands stayed on the wheel until Louise spoke again.

"It was 1975, in August," Louise said, "when he came in one day and said he felt tired. He'd been swimming at Piney Lake and walked a long way home. He was so hot. I told him to sleep for an hour or two before supper. And I told him . . . ," her voice grew slower as though she were trying to remember, though Molly knew even as she told it that she was trying not to remember and that she remembered it all every day.

"And so he did. He went upstairs and I called up once to see if he wanted a glass of milk or juice or something, if he was thirsty, but he said he wasn't. I remember how he called back down to me."

Louise turned to Molly now. She hadn't looked at her since she started telling this. "He opened the door to his room and called down, 'Not right now,' and when he said it, Molly, I've never told this to anyone but Sig, but when he said it, I got a chill inside and I said, 'Are you sure?' the chill so definite that I wanted to say something else, or have him say something else. It made no sense to feel like 'Not right now' meant that there might be no other time but 'right now.' It was that part that bored into me as I went back to the kitchen.

"He never answered me when I said, 'Are you sure?' He didn't hear, because when he slept he always turned on a fan. He liked the noise of a fan when he slept. Even in winter he turned it on." Louise smiled, but her mouth looked like the mouth of a cat. Molly's face grew tight with listening.

"And I fixed supper. I remember what I fixed exactly, because the feeling stayed with me all the way through the preparing. Roast beef with a dark gravy, green beans, and a large bowl of mashed potatoes. He loved those things. Some cheese. And I had ice cream for dessert. Once I went up to his room and went in." She slowed the telling and Molly could see she let herself see him again, his face sleeping. "And he was fine then. Just sleeping normally. I went back down and thought how silly and dramatic I was, how I would tell Sig of my foolishness.

"I finished cooking and Sig came in. I told him and clutched again in that icy place inside myself. Because what was going on inside me did not seem foolish, and I felt glad I wasn't going up the steps like Sig was doing. I was glad I wasn't going, and held the spoon over the sink to wash, but I didn't turn on the water. I waited until Sig went all the way into the room, until he had a moment to tell Joel to get up and to turn off the fan. Another moment, and I held the spoon under the faucet, my hand ready to turn it on, but I wasn't looking at it. I wasn't looking at anything, and Sig yelled *Louise*. Once. Just like that."

She told Molly how the doctors talked about the poison in Joel's body. "It might have been a bee sting, something he was allergic to. He just stopped breathing. He had got so hot." She told the whole thing in practically one piece, in places going slower, and her eyes so open to memory that Molly could hardly look at her.

"So I know what you've lost."

Then she said something directed, not to Molly, but to herself, though it entered Molly and connected her completely. "I know what it is," she said, "to find a shirt, to see the stains not washed out, and oh, the creases around the shoulders that were made by his arms."

Lucas came outside to see why they were sitting in the car. He'd seen them drive up. "What's the matter?" he said when he saw their faces.

"We're just talking," Louise told him. She walked with him to the house and told him she had some new children at the farm and one of the horses was about to foal. She said he should come out there to see them.

"Can I?" Lucas turned to his mother.

"I don't see why not," Molly said.

Frank Bates prepared meals, as he had been doing for three weeks. It was the middle of August, and he spoke now about going home.

"Who'll cook when you go?" Molly said.

He leafed through Evelyn's cookbooks to find recipes marked "good" or "delicious." They had even tried a few marked "fair," but no one liked those dishes much. Tonight he prepared a veal cutlet and Molly warned him that Lucas and Franci might not try it unless he said it was like chicken. Molly told them everything was "like chicken."

"You've got to eat more," her father told her. Molly had lost ten pounds so quickly that her face was pale and looked pressed down.

"I'm not hungry."

"I know you're not," he said without patience, "but you've got to eat anyway." He set two bowls on the counter and dished out some frozen lemon yogurt, which he knew Molly loved. "Sit down a minute."

"I don't want any."

"Just a little," he said. She took the spoon he handed to her. He had on an apron. "It's like chicken," he said.

CHAPTER
TEN

A few days before Molly's mother went into the hospital for the last time, Molly took her to shop for a dress. It was an overcast day, and her mother said, "Molly, you're going to think this is a strange request . . ."

She wanted to go shopping. Molly didn't see how it could be done, so Evelyn Bates explained that if she got into the wheelchair and if they moved slowly, they could go to the mall and buy a dress she could be buried in. At first Molly said no.

"It's a long time to wear a dress you don't like, Molly." So Molly went to the closet and got the wheelchair. "We can't tell your father," Evelyn said.

"Why not?"

"He wouldn't let us go. He'd be horribly stubborn about it, and I'm not strong enough to fight him now."

Evelyn Bates pushed herself up and threw her legs off the bed. "Help me get dressed," she said. She got stronger as she talked about it. "I wish my hair were clean." She sprinkled powder on her hair and brushed it through to get rid of the greasy look that comes from lying on a pillow all day. The phone rang just as they closed the front door and Molly ran to answer it.

"No. We're fine. No. You stay there. Mom is sleeping. No." When she hung up, they giggled and felt that a remarkable quality of mischief had been added to their life.

They decided to go to Belk's because it was at the far end of the mall, easy to get in and out of. As they drove, Evelyn Bates could not realize how things had changed, and Molly thought of how long it had been since her life was normal.

"It never occurred to me you might want to do this," Molly said. The doors to Belk's opened automatically, and they both felt committed to the experience.

"We'll have to pick a color I won't get tired of," Evelyn Bates said. A saleswoman came over.

"We're looking for a dress," Molly told her.

"Any special occasion?"

"Yes." Evelyn was about to say more.

"It's for a dance," said Molly, and pointed to her mother. They laughed, but the saleswoman didn't know whether she should laugh or not. The name tag on her dress read Carla. Carla couldn't guess the mood of these two women. They picked out dresses and brought them to the dressing room.

It took both Carla and Molly to pull off Evelyn's skirt. She stood to let them pull it down, around her knees, but her knees collapsed and she sat quickly. She sat on Carla's hand and grew tickled. Carla was shocked.

"I'm all right," she said to Carla. She wanted Carla to think she was crippled rather than dying. She pointed to a dress with tiny flowers that she knew she wouldn't like, but said anyway, "I'll try that one."

"What ki-ind of dance?" Carla said slowly. Evelyn Bates pulled the flowered dress over her head. She looked like an animal fighting in a sack.

The third dress was one Carla picked out—white linen with blue collar and cuffs. "A little more expensive than the others," she said, but Molly knew when she saw her mother's face that this was the dress.

Carla brought in two more dresses to try. She wanted to sell more than one. "You'll need this one for the fall," she said, and held up a light wool plaid.

"I don't think so," said Evelyn, and she was perfectly serious.

"So, what did you two do today?" Frank Bates asked when he got home. Molly brought him a drink.

"Bought a dress."

"Well, let's see it." He thought Molly had bought one for herself.

Evelyn came in wearing her new white linen. She looked like a bride, and they didn't tell him it was for her funeral. They just let him stand there like old times and see his wife in a dress she'd bought to wear somewhere. He loved the moment and didn't get sad when it was over. In fact, the whole night and all the next day, he kept thinking of Evelyn looking so slight and lovely and pale in her dress.

"I love the collar," he said, because he had learned over the years to name something he liked about what she was wearing. Evelyn was convinced, when he said something specific, that she looked beautiful. "You are beautiful," he said.

Molly thought of this because she didn't know how her own children would remember her or Will when they grew older. She didn't know what they would think when she told them the divorce was final. She didn't know how to ask them to understand.

Zack's place in the woods had no electricity, but he had a coal-oil heater and some Coleman lamps that gave light. Molly had never been to where he lived. She went there today partly because she hadn't spoken to him much since the day he came to her house and partly because she knew he was in town for the weekend. She had seen him at the gas station. His face these days looked alert to speculation about the very worth of himself.

Molly knew where his shack was; everyone knew. As she went through the woods, a small part of her mind expected to find Joe there. She saw the two-room shed and decided not to go in. It was late morning. There were chairs outside the front screen door and a library book on one of them. Zack walked out.

"Did Joe ever come here?" she asked him.

Zack lifted the book and opened it to the back cover. He showed her the due date and she smiled. She knew Joe had brought it to him.

"A few times," he told her, and sat in the other chair.

The sun was not high, and they could hear the stream.

"When will you go back to the farm?"

"Tomorrow. I would've seen you before I left." He held the book in his lap. His shoulders had a meek pride. He was the kind of man who had never done anything remotely easy.

"Joe used to sit over there." He pointed to a stump and Molly knew just how Joe would look sitting there. She sat suspended in the thought of him.

A partly dug trench beside the house was filled with water. Molly didn't ask what it was for. By silent consent neither of them spoke. They sat seeing the light move higher and had an urgent readiness to be transformed.

Louise called the next week and asked them to a pig roast. Zack and Sig would roast the pig in a big oil drum. "Come early and stay all day," Louise said. She told Molly to bring Ben, but Molly didn't know how to be with Ben now. Sometimes she didn't even return his calls.

Lucas and Franci counted the days until the pig roast. They marked off time on the calendar, and liked the idea of going to Louise and Sig's.

"Is it an orphanage?" Franci asked.

"No. Their parents are in jail or sick, but don't ask them about it, not unless they bring it up themselves."

"I won't ask *any*body *any*thing," said Lucas.

Saturday was hot. The sultry heat of August was upon them, but there was a breeze at the farm. Molly could see Louise at the kitchen door watching them drive toward the house. With her were the twins, who had arrived the day before. They were five years old, and Louise introduced them. "Matt and Libby," she said. Matt held onto Louise's hand, but Libby stood alone.

Sig called to them from the shed. "It's nearly ready." Zack was brushing the pig with a sauce.

A long table inside the shed was draped with tablecloths. Plates and glasses were in place. Martha put napkins on each plate and tried to keep the boys away from the huge platter of brownies. A bowl of hushpuppies sat uncovered and Tony kept coming in to help himself. The hushpuppies were fried in a deep skillet beneath the drum and placed hot in the big bowl.

"Quit taking everything," Martha yelled at Tony and Carlos. She spoke with the weariness of someone who has said those words all day. Fifteen children grew strong now under Louise and Sig's care.

Before everyone sat down to eat, Louise reached into the top shelf of the cabinet and took down something Carlos and Tony had been waiting for. "Don't fight about this anymore," Louise told them. The item was silver and looked as though it had been found outside—some broken thing kids know how to treasure.

Sig served the feast. He wore a chef's hat and shorts and a T-shirt. Zack helped with the cooking and did other chores, but he still wasn't part of them yet. He was like a small, torn remnant that couldn't be used.

It was almost four o'clock, and Molly sat on the front steps talking to Louise, when Carlos came running around the side of the house. "Quick, come quick!" His voice was urgent. "Sig's at the barn. That spotted mare is having her foal. He said to tell you *now*."

Louise rolled her eyes. "I knew it," she said, and got up to follow him. She motioned for Franci and Lucas to come. "You ever seen a new foal?"

They shook their heads, their eyes bright with confusion.

"It comes out like this," she said, and placed her arms straight down by her sides, her face pushed upward.

"Ga!" Lucas was stung with the thought of it.

"Quick!" Carlos ran ahead of them, and though Molly didn't believe the foal would be born by the time they got there, she ran any-way.

When they got to the barn, they found Sig sitting beside the sprawled horse. He stroked her neck and spoke in a soft voice, like a confession. He told Louise that the nose of the foal had broken through, but they couldn't see anything yet.

What came first was a large white bubble, the size of a soccer ball—a thick film that burst with water. The children laughed when it burst, but their laughter grew short as they saw the nose poke out, coming fast, the head and then the shoulders coming slower.

Louise asked all the children if they had ever seen anything like this, and she put the question to them as though this was a welcome thing. "That foal is coming out so easy," she said. And just then the shoulders came through, popping almost, and the spotted mare punched and stretched her neck.

"What's she doing that for?" somebody asked.

"She's trying to get it out." There was blood, and the twins backed away. Sig told them the foal would be fine. "It'll be standing up in a few hours, stumbling around, and you'll think it's so funny." The children looked at Sig, because they didn't want to look at the horse. They laughed when he said how funny it would be. They hoped that was true.

The foal dived out now, headfirst into the hay, with a shiny blue placenta like a plastic sheet wrapped around it. Loose in places, it blurred the shape. Sig started to pull off some of the film, but Zack lifted it, and the rest of the amniotic fluid spilled out. Zack said he had done this kind of work before and knew how to take care of horses better than anything else. He didn't say where he'd learned this.

The hay beneath the mare was matted thick. Zack smoothed a place for the foal. It jerked and tried to arrange itself, having room now to move. It looked free and scared.

"Can it see?" Franci asked, because she remembered how the baby foxes couldn't see for a couple of days.

"It can see fine."

When the foal came out, everyone clapped and cheered. The cord stayed connected for an hour or two while the foal got enough nourishment. "Then the mother stands up," Sig says, "and she breaks it." The foal squirmed and began to move its legs.

"See?" said Louise. "It won't be long now." The young kids laughed and danced their own legs around.

"Louise and Sig taught us everything," Lucas said on the way home. They reached the house after dark. Zack had wanted to return with them but decided to stay with the foal. He cleaned the stall and rubbed down the mare. The foal was standing and wobbly before they left.

That night Molly woke to hear Franci talking in her sleep. She went to Franci's room and saw her sitting up in bed, addressing a wall. Franci didn't see her mother, even when Molly sat on the bed beside her. She kept saying Joe's name.

A week ago Franci had told her mother, "Mama, sometimes I see things, and hear things. I dream something and think it's real." She didn't know how much she should say, and was trying to make it sound ordinary.

"Like what, honey?"

"Like Joe. I see Joe sometimes."

Everybody in the house believed in spirits now, so Molly didn't move or flinch. Instead she talked as though they were speaking of corn. "When did you see him?"

Franci didn't want her to believe too much. "He wasn't real," she said. "But it seemed like he was, I mean," and she looked out, not seeing the window or even the reflection of them talking, but seeing Joe as she had seen him earlier. "It was a cold dream, but it seemed so real when it happened."

Molly longed to see whatever that dream was. "Did he say anything?"

"No. But he looked at me, Mama, looked straight at me, and then I woke up." They were silent, almost reverent, then Molly said, "Well, honey, you were lucky to see that. It's nothing to be afraid of."

"Was it really Joe, or what?"

"I don't know. Maybe."

"Don't tell Lucas or anybody."

"I won't," Molly promised, but the next day she broke her promise and told William.

"What do you *mean* she saw him? Does she think she *saw* him?"

"Well, no, Will. I just told you so you'd know what was going on."

"I don't know, Molly. It doesn't seem right to me."

To hear Franci call out to Joe as though he stood in the room made Molly long to be inside Franci's head no matter what the cost. She wanted to spend the night seeing him, and hearing him talk. Franci started awake, her eyes wide like an invalid's.

"Franci, honey? Did you see him?"

Franci nodded.

"Did he say anything?" It was so easy to believe these things in the middle of the night. Molly wanted the possibility of it to be true. She wiped Franci's mouth where there was a small amount of drool at the corners.

"He talked."

"What did he say?" It felt bizarre to ask this.

"He said that we should . . ." but she didn't tell what she heard. She started crying. "I didn't know what to do, Mama."

Molly waited to see if she might say more, then said, "I love you, Franci."

"Mama?"

"What?"

"What does it mean? Am I going to dream some more?"

"You might. Yes." Molly didn't say how much she wished to have those dreams, how she wanted to hear his voice, just once.

"Mama, will he come back?"

"No, honey."

"Will we see him?"

"No. You might dream awhile longer, but then you'll probably give that up too."

"Will you stay in my room a little while?"

"Yes."

"Will you rub my back?"

Before Molly slept again, she pulled open the curtains in her room. She stood, she didn't know how long, looking out the window. The trees absorbed the hot night air. They grew dark at the middle. Mist in the yard was shaped like a boat at first, then like an egg. Molly wanted to offer some supplication to the room, or sky, but she couldn't think of what to say. She lay down. The only light was coming from a nearby streetlamp, and it carved a field of vision in her room, slender columns that acted as moorings to her slow mind. And she thought to herself, though finally she spoke it out loud: I need to know so much more than I do.

The next morning the sky was the color of copper and zinc, and for one moment it seemed that nothing at all had happened in Molly Hanner's life. It had been almost four weeks, and Molly counted each day without Joe as though she were counting toward something instead of counting back to the time when she had him. And she pictured herself in the future saying, "Ten years ago today . . ." or "Thirty-five years ago last week . . ." and measuring her life by that meaning.

Molly pulled her robe around her. She wouldn't wake Franci and Lucas. She would let them sleep until noon, if they wanted.

The sun came into her kitchen full of honey and bright surfaces, the way it does in an Andrew Wyeth painting. It came in as though she were remembering rather than seeing it. She opened the back door to let in the morning air, and in the short time it had taken her to come downstairs, the sky had changed from zinc to complete daylight.

Last week Franci and Lucas finally took what they wanted from Joe's room. They were shy about choosing, but Molly took the pennant off the wall and handed it to Franci, then she gave Lucas the skateboard hanging in Joe's closet. They spent two hours going through pictures and Joe's clothes. When they left, the room looked different, finished.

Molly placed a filter in the coffeepot and poured in fresh coffee. She could see a young man coming down the road toward the house. The window over the kitchen table showed him clearly. He was coming this way.

Three boys had come by in the past week. It was the time of year when boys sold magazines or household cleaners or small miracle brushes that could clean places Molly didn't even care about having clean. One boy walked now in the shadows of trees. He looked like Joe. Two of the ones last week looked like Joe as they came to the house, until they got close. It happened all the time now. Molly would be driving along and somebody about Joe's height would cross the street, jaywalking, running quickly somewhere, and his hair—the way it stood up in back—or the way he ran looked just like Joe, until her heartbeat felt fragile, like wings.

The perking sound of the coffee was a comfort to her and she decided not to invite the boy in, not even to answer the door. He could come back later. He carried a briefcase or something with his sale-ables in it. She would not buy anything.

The boy walked straight to the house, and Molly wanted to complain to someone about the number of salesmen who could come by in one month. The hair, the stride, the slope of his shoulders looked like Joe. *Damn.* The other day, when she thought that, after the boy left she'd felt tired and run down. She got up to stand beside the coffeemaker, so he wouldn't see her at the table. He would think no one was up yet, or that they were busy. She would not answer the door. She was tired. She could see him from the window as he came up the back steps.

And Molly hated God, at that moment she hated God and even said it in a low, prayerlike tone: *I hate you for this*, as though God had added personally to her grief by sending this boy. "I hate you," she said a little louder.

She filled her cup and leaned over the sink. She wouldn't look out again. Her eyes could stay closed until he was gone. She put down her cup and waited.

But then she heard what she thought was a knock, though it

wasn't. It was the screen door opening, and the young man came in. He walked straight into the house and saw his mother at the sink.

Her eyes were closed so she wouldn't have to look, but when she opened them, her hands began to flutter in the sink, and her whole body rushed with the upward wash of a hundred birds.

"Mom?" he said.

CHAPTER
ELEVEN

William was sitting on the deck of his apartment when the phone rang. It rang twice, but he didn't reach it before the ringing stopped.

He started back to his chair. A half-eaten peach lay open with the swell of seed in the middle that made him feel oversexed when he looked at it. He thought of Carol and wondered if she'd been the one who called.

The phone rang again. This time it rang until he answered.

"Will?"

"Molly?" Her voice sounded funny to him. "What's wrong?"

"I need to come over there."

"Now?" Molly had only been to his apartment three times. "Why, Molly?"

"Something has happened."

William couldn't refuse her tone. "Okay," he said.

She hung up and William felt a chill move up, not down, his spine. Molly didn't sound demanding, nor was it a plea. It was just that something had happened that he must know about. He checked the apartment for items belonging to Carol. Molly's phone call didn't seem to have anything to do with them personally, but he was afraid it had everything to do with their happiness.

Molly couldn't tell William on the phone. He needed to see Joe standing before him as she had done, because even seeing him, she couldn't believe it. She hadn't been able to believe his death; now she couldn't believe his life. She watched every move as he got into the car, and she kept touching his arm. She didn't know what to say.

"Why didn't you go to your dad's first?" she asked, pleased in her heart that he had come home to her.

"I did," said Joe. "I mean, I called him. He didn't answer." Joe's eyes had another spirit in them and Molly wondered what kind of man he would be. She thought that probably for a long time he wouldn't be able to trust anyone.

In the parking lot of William's apartment complex, Molly told Joe to wait in the car for just a few minutes before he came up the steps. She wanted to go in first and prepare William for what he was about to see. She couldn't help remembering the night they spent in the belief that Joe was alive, as though something magic had happened from that.

"Molly, I don't know what this is about," William began when he opened the door. He felt intruded upon and told her so.

"What do you mean, Will? I've never *done* this before. You act like I'm always doing this!"

"That time you brought Lucas and Franci!" he reminded her.

"But I didn't *ask* to come over. God, Will, I just brought them here. *You* asked me in!" Molly stood just inside his doorway, and she could hear Joe coming up behind her now.

"Will!" Molly yelled at him. They were arguing. They had not been together two minutes, and they were arguing. "Will! Listen!"

William's expression showed that he could see Joe on the steps behind her, but there was no understanding in what he saw. She took hold of his arm and said quickly, under her breath as though she should whisper something that was too important to say out loud,

"It's Joe, Will, it *is* Joe. And he's all right. He's here and he's all right."

Joe stood in the doorway now behind his parents, so Molly moved to the side and let him step in toward his father. William didn't move, so Joe began to explain how he didn't know about the car crash or about Andrew and Roy, how he'd run away for these few weeks. He hadn't meant to stay so long. But William didn't hear any of what he said. He didn't know how to test whether or not this was a dream.

William had dreamed of Joe standing before him, as close as this, and each time, if he reached, the vision disappeared. He'd dreamed it enough times that even in the dream he had learned not to touch or reach out, so that Joe could stay longer in front of him. But now William broke the dream decision and reached, and when he touched Joe's shoulder and heard his words, the whole reality of it seemed doubled.

William almost never prayed, so his prayer now seemed numb and stupid. And his smile at that moment was close to a disfigurement.

He didn't want the vision to disperse into smoke. He wanted what stood before him to be simply true. He still hadn't said anything, so Molly said, "Will?" but before she got it out, Joe stepped forward, all the way, and William held him until he was transformed back into the commonness of things.

Lucas and Franci couldn't take their eyes off Joe.

When Molly came upstairs that morning to wake them, they didn't know why they had to get up so early.

"How come?" Franci argued, when Molly opened the curtains. "You said we could sleep late." Molly scooted her into Joe's room, where Lucas slept.

"Lucas?"

"Huh?"

"Wake up!"

"What's the matter?" He looked to Franci and she shrugged.

"It's something good, something better than you can imagine." Molly's tone of voice put them into expectation of what they might imagine, and they woke completely.

"What is it!" Franci said.

"It's a surprise!" Molly said. "It's about Joe!"

"You found him?" Franci's face grew grim, because finding Joe meant an end to her hope. She couldn't imagine why it would be a good thing, except that she knew her mother talked about her need for a final service.

"And he's all right," Molly said, but Franci didn't hear this or didn't hear it so that it registered, because her face when she saw Joe come in the door was still sad, and stayed sad a few seconds after Lucas had already jumped up to grab Joe's waist. And though Franci smiled and looked straight at him, she couldn't move, so he moved to her. But before he spoke to anyone, Joe said, "Hey! What happened to my room!"

It was not until a little later that Molly called her father. She had to tell him three times that Joe was alive. Later, he said he was so confused with the information that, in his gladness about Joe, he hoped maybe Evelyn might come back too. He said he believed for a moment that anything could happen.

It was the middle of the afternoon and they sat at Molly's kitchen table. Neighbors and friends came by the house to see Joe. The newspaper took pictures and the kitchen was full of people. Joe told them where he had been. He had more food in front of him than he could possibly eat. It was as if everyone thought he had been someplace that didn't have food.

Earlier, Joe had told the story to his parents and to Franci and Lucas. William and Molly said, "Why? Why did you do it?" They forgot he didn't know about the death of his friends.

"On the night of Franci's party, I snuck out," Joe said. "I went to Dad's first, then to Andrew's house."

"But I don't understand why you never called to tell us anything."

"I *did* call." He turned to Franci. "I talked to Franci and she said you and Mom had gone somewhere." They remembered Franci telling them the next morning how Joe called last night and said he would be gone for a while. No one asked the exact time of the call because their shock of sadness didn't allow them to exercise a logical reasoning. It was one of those moments that could have made all the difference, but the moment slipped by unnoticed. "We played cards about an hour, until Roy and Andrew said they wanted to get pizza. I left with them. I offered to drive and had even left the keys in my car, but Andrew said he wanted to drive, so I got in the back seat. I remember I took my coat off." He turned toward everyone as though this were an explanation of something.

"Anyway, Andrew started toward Black Mountain and I said they were going wrong. They laughed and said they were going right, and it was Black Mountain they were headed for. I knew I didn't want to do that. For one thing, they'd met two girls a few weeks before and were always wanting to go over there. I got mad and said if they wanted to go, they shouldn't have brought me. I said to let me out.

"There was a Holiday Inn on a hill. I could see it, so I told them to take me there. I'd call somebody to bring my car. I think Andrew was relieved to get rid of me. They let me out at the bottom of the hill. It was eleven-fifteen, because I looked at my watch."

The night had been muggy, too hot for hurrying up that hill, and though Joe didn't tell anyone this part, he imagined himself staying all night at the Holiday Inn, and as he passed the swimming pool he thought that if he'd just worn his old blue shorts he could've used them to swim in.

The days at the beach had broken something. Joe couldn't forget what it had felt like when he came back from the beach and heard William say how he missed him. William had asked Joe to come over, said they could rent a movie and cook some steaks. So Joe went to bed that night in his father's apartment, and he felt like a man again. He couldn't feel like a man at home.

And Joe asked his father that night, calling out the question from the bathroom because he didn't want to seem demanding, asked if he could move in with him completely. He wanted more than this part-time basis.

The silence that followed let Joe know that the question had been taken seriously. "You can," William said, his voice tentative. He came around the corner of the bathroom. "But we'll need to wait a few months. Maybe by the time school starts." But that seemed to Joe a very long wait.

"I want you here." William sat on the edge of the tub. They both wore pajama bottoms that belonged to William but were dirty because he kept forgetting to wash them. "I *do* want you here."

The Holiday Inn desk clerk asked Joe for a credit card, and though he hadn't decided to stay overnight, when he took out the card it seemed decided for him. A banquet room to the left of the lobby was set up with long tables. It was late and the food had been picked over, but the clerk said he could have "all he wanted for $4.50." It would be put on his bill.

Joe piled his plate with the Holiday Inn food, and when the waitress came to see what he wanted to drink, he wondered if she thought he was older. He imagined people around him might think he was a salesman or something, and if anyone asked, he might tell them he was.

It was almost midnight when Joe, settled in his room, decided to call home. He would say he was at Andrew's. When he dialed, a girl—not Franci—answered and Joe said, "Franci?" so the girl called Franci to the phone. "Tell Mom I'm staying at Andrew's tonight. Is she asleep?"

"She's not here."

"Where is she?"

"Dad came over. They went somewhere."

"Listen," he told Franci, "I might go off for a few days. Tell them not to worry. I might just . . ."

"Joe, I've got to *go!*" Franci wanted to get back to her party.

"I just wanted to tell you."

"What?" There were so many noises in the background. Something had dropped.

"I just wanted you to tell Mom."

"*Okay!*"

Joe had called home. He wasn't even sure then where he would go, but during dinner he thought of going to Jenny's house in Florida. He had visited her and her brother last summer, and their family said to come back any time. So he thought of getting money from the automatic teller in the morning. He would ride the bus to Jenny's. He might stay a week, or maybe longer, so that when he came back the shock of his going would bring the family back together. He believed he could make it happen like that and saw it before him as a happy ending to a story.

After he talked to Franci, he decided to watch a movie. He took off his clothes, lay down naked outside the covers, and propped himself up with pillows from both beds. He could see himself in the mirror and felt heroic lying there.

"Jenny helped me get a job at a gas station and I stayed the first week with her family. Then I moved in with her brother. He has an apartment. I called a few times to tell you where I was, but no one answered." This was only partly true.

"What did you think we would do?" William said.

Joe didn't answer his father's question, but Molly, looking at Joe's face, answered William. "He thought," Molly said, "that if he left, we might get back together. Didn't you, Joe? You thought it might change everything back, didn't you?"

"Is that right? Is that what you thought?" William's face looked as if it might explode into a thousand filmy strands.

"Sort of." His idea seemed foolish now, and his heart quite literally hurt with the thought of what he had done.

Joe talked all afternoon, but he didn't tell them everything. He didn't tell them about the long bus ride where he sat with two boys about his age who got on at Columbia. He didn't say how he'd called his dad's apartment, and when William answered he knew nothing had changed. So he stayed another week, and another, trying to make something happen. He'd hung up the phone without saying anything.

Jenny guessed it. "Your parents don't know where you are, do they?"

"No."

"I thought so. You should call them."

"I did. Twice." He didn't tell Jenny that no one answered and that the time he called his dad, he hung up.

"You should call again," Jenny said.

"I'm going home tomorrow." It was a decision made at that second. It had been almost four weeks.

Joe had called his dad from the bus station in Stringer's Ridge, but he decided to take a taxi to the edge of the park near his house and walk from there.

As he went down the road, he could see that the kitchen door was open, so he knew his mother was awake. He'd eaten a greasy breakfast, and his stomach hurt. He wore shirts and shorts Jenny's brother had given him, and he had everything else in the small bag he'd bought at a thrift shop. He tried to decide if he was in love with Jenny and thought he probably was. He didn't know why, but it didn't feel the way he thought love should feel.

When he opened the screen door, he saw his mother at the sink. She had her eyes closed and Joe almost didn't recognize her. He almost thought she was somebody else. Her face looked like a mask, until he spoke.

"Should I go see Andrew's family or Roy's mother?" Joe asked them before he went to bed.

"I don't know," William told him. "Maybe not just yet."

Molly restored Joe's room to its former order. Could she say how it was to do this? The bedspread was back on the bed. His trophies and box of arrowheads, his shirts and pants and robe—all back in order.

She starched the curtains from his room and hung them. She folded his underwear neatly in the drawers and put the razor and cream in the bathroom for him. When she opened the door in the mornings, she saw the cat sleeping there. She could not speak or breathe. And for the first few nights William slept on the couch downstairs because he could not bear to go to his apartment.

"Why'd you do it?" Franci sat in the front seat beside Joe. He was taking her to her piano lesson.

"I didn't just _do_ it. I mean, I didn't think it out like that. I just left."

They rode in silence. "But we thought you were dead." She spoke as if Joe hadn't understood her question. He might be apologizing for this the rest of his life. Some people thought Joe should be punished and that Molly and William should think of something appropriate. But Molly knew they would never think of anything.

"I had to get out," he said. "I wasn't thinking of anything. Nothing else was in my mind."

"I know," said Franci. "You never even gave me a birthday present."

Joe laughed. Franci laughed too, but she didn't know what was funny.

Joe's friends admired him, said it was awesome the way he had come back and blown everyone away. "Man!" they said in complete admiration. "Man!" One boy told Joe that he had thought about doing the same thing when his parents split up, but he was an only child and finally couldn't do it.

School started in two weeks, so Molly took Lucas and Franci to buy school supplies. They loved to see the neat rows of paper and packages of pens. They had already been assigned teachers. Franci had six teachers, but Lucas had the teacher everyone dreaded getting in the fifth grade. There were legendary stories of her meanness, and both Joe and Franci had been in her class. Lucas complained about his year ahead with Mrs. Gastes, but his complaints were also bragging. No one forgot that Mrs. Gastes taught the smart

ones, and Lucas had been afraid he might not make it into her class.
He picked a notebook with Dallas Cowboys on the front and carried
all his supplies on it like a tray.

"Mama says there's an eclipse tonight. She's gonna make us watch
it." Lucas knew he should complain but looked forward to it. This
was the first week in September.

"What eclipse?" asked Franci. She hated it when Lucas told her
something she had no idea about.

"It's tonight and Ben's coming over."

"What time?" She planned to object, but sounded as excited as
Lucas.

"Two-thirty."

"Do we have to?"

"She *said*."

Molly came in to see how well they had cleaned their rooms.
They were required to clean off their desks before school started
again.

"Do we *have* to watch the eclipse?" Franci didn't want her to in-
spect the room yet.

"Don't you want to?"

"Not much. I wish it weren't in the middle of the night."

Molly looked around the room. "You'll still be working on this
room at the rate you're going."

"We have to, don't we?" Lucas said. It was a statement.

"Yes." Molly picked up clothes and threw them into the hamper.
"Joe too?"

"Yes." The inclusion of Joe silenced them. They figured it must
be important if he agreed to do it.

"I knew all the time that Joe was okay," Franci told Lucas. "I mean,
that he was all right somewhere." They had finished cleaning their
rooms and had taken Joe's things back to him. Joe let Franci keep the
pennant and Lucas the skateboard.

"What do you mean?" They hadn't been talking about Joe when she said this.

"I mean, when they said he'd died in the car crash, I knew it wasn't true. You know how you know something like that. I just *knew*."

"No you didn't."

"I did!" Franci reached for her diary and opened it to the page dated the day after the car crash. She read it aloud to Lucas. Lucas was so surprised at her reading to him from her diary that he almost forgot to listen. He felt privileged. He felt that what he was about to hear would be so secret and portentous that his mind, instead of remaining focused, became distracted by the importance of listening.

"Joe was killed today," she read coldly, "when a car with Roy Mathis and Andrew Hawkins went off the bridge into the French Broad River." She had tried to word it like a newspaper article. "I don't think he's dead though. I really don't think he is." Franci looked up to see Lucas' expression. "See?" She spoke as though this were absolute proof of her prescience. "I knew he was alive then. I felt it."

"That's nothing," said Lucas, unconvinced. "You could've meant he was alive somewhere, like in *heaven* or something. You could've meant that *easy*."

"I *didn't* though." Franci read part of it again, emphasizing certain words to convince him.

"Did you tell anybody?" Lucas asked in a pointed way, because he was sure if she had thought this was true then she would have told it, and if she didn't tell then it meant she didn't really believe it. "You didn't tell *us*."

Franci grew silent.

"What else did you say in there?" Lucas wanted Franci to read more, because he'd been curious about her diary. He'd seen it beside her bed and once tried to pry it open. Franci kept it locked, but Lucas found a key in a dish on her dresser. If he had a diary (which he knew he would never have), he would put in it things he did each day but wouldn't write down anything he thought about. He would never put his thoughts on paper, even if he kept it locked. So as Franci read to him, his ideas about physical bravery changed, because he knew he could not measure up to her kind of courage.

"Eclipses happen a lot," Ben told them at dinner. "It's just that we're not always able to see them."

He began to explain to Lucas and Franci, using oranges and grapefruit and a flashlight, how the sun, the moon, and the earth pass each other so that the shadow blocks out the moon.

Franci called Caroline over to make cookies for the eclipse, and Lucas studied what Ben had explained. He thought of telling it to his class when school started. When they made him write about what he did last summer, he would write about the eclipse, or else about Joe's dying.

Ben wanted Molly to come back with him to his house. He had missed seeing her over the chaotic weeks since the accident. It had been so long since they were together, he said.

Molly hadn't told Ben about the night she spent with William. She pretended she never even thought about it, but whenever she saw Ben she thought of how she hadn't told him. It seemed strange to feel she had cheated on Ben with her own husband. Everything was backwards now. And she even imagined Ben wouldn't care.

"I love you, Molly." He had said it before he meant to, and both of them looked shocked. They sat on the sofa in his house, but Molly couldn't return his words, though she meant them in her heart. She had held, since those moments at the beach, the jagged curve of his brown head in her mind. He turned her blouse down her arms and slipped off her skirt.

They touched each other like blind people learning everything for the first time, and his hands handled her feet as though he bathed them. He said again that he loved her, repeating it because he wanted her to know from the fullness of his voice what he meant.

When he took off his clothes, Molly saw that he was more manly than she had imagined. His firm arms and legs were muscled from sports in his youth, but as he looked at her he didn't smile. Molly examined his face for a trace of indulgence. He frowned at something beyond her. Neither of them made a sound. A faint sour smell came from one of them, Molly didn't know which.

Ben looked quite mad and sulky, a mood Molly hadn't seen in him before. But it was not sulkiness at all, just the full, thick-skinned idea of having a moment without language or measurement. He didn't know the strength of his own unease—how it affected Molly. He almost seemed to stagger, even though he lay on top of her and his face shone without dissimulation, like a small lamp.

He stayed a long time inside Molly and let her come, then again, staying, composing for her a wide open light, and when it was over Molly thought he could teach her to extend her way in the world, and she measured this against her life.

He took her home and they waited until time for the eclipse. They felt mischievous, like teenagers who had burned down the town and were sure people spoke rumors about them.

"It's started," Ben told them, and he set the telescope so each could look at the small dark line at the edge of the moon. As more of it became darker, they sat on the driveway to see the whole dramatic effect. It didn't seem like shadow, but more than shadow—like a big, coarse bird. When it had been half canceled, Lucas asked, "What will it do now?" as though he inquired about the end of a movie. It had a coppery red glow.

Ben's explanation of the eclipse had almost nothing to do with the experience of watching it. Compared to the experience, the explanation seemed irrelevant, except for memory and statement.

"The shadow keeps going," Ben told him. "Then after the eclipse, it seems like everything stops for a moment. That the whole universe just quits, and everything is still, waiting to see if it'll get back to normal again. The birds, all the stars, no sound, just like the start of a quick gasp. It's like somebody seeing the ocean for the first time. You can't stop thinking about it."

None of them could say exactly what it was like to watch it. They could see stars they hadn't seen before. Ben pointed out the new stars to them. It took a long time for the shadow to pass.

"People used to watch this and die of fright," Molly told them. "They thought it was a dragon eating the moon."

"Well, that would do it for me." Joe got up and went back to bed before it was over. Everyone else stayed until the end.

The next day began badly. Molly woke sick and the fox had escaped by digging a hole under the fence during the night. Franci was inconsolable and locked herself in her room.

Louise came to town in the late afternoon and brought a load of fresh vegetables. The twins were with her.

"How is Zack?" Molly asked.

"Ten years younger than when he came. He takes care of the horses for us, and Sig's teaching him to run the tractors and repair them. He grew these vegetables." Louise told Molly she looked awful and sent the twins to look for Franci.

"She's in her room," said Molly. She pulled a pack of cigarettes from her shirt pocket and told Louise about the fox. She apologized and confessed in the same breath about not smoking for almost ten years. "Since Lucas was born. I smoked when I was pregnant." She lit her cigarette and blew the smoke to one side. "Will this bother you?"

"So," Louise's face carried the whole question to Molly's head, "are you pregnant now?"

Molly had missed her period in August, but she thought that had to do with the strain of losing Joe. Now it was September and she had missed this month too.

"Louise!" She exhaled again, and didn't look anywhere but straight ahead. She knew when it had been conceived. Her lips grew tight as she spoke. "It's probably nothing," she said. "It's probably nothing at all." She put out the cigarette.

The night Molly had spent with William, they slept in each other's arms, and during that time Molly experienced the phenomenon she experienced with each of her children. It was this: on the night of conception, a few minutes before sleep came, Molly heard a clear, single-timbred note, like that of an oboe. Like praise. That night she sat straight up and said, "No, Will."

"What's the matter?" William sat up too. He had forgotten where he was.

"Nothing. A dream."

The next morning she left early, and the regular grief of the day came back. Once, though, during that morning, she thought of the note that woke her, as clear as two lines crossing through a distance, converging to make a perfect point—bringing the world of stupid praise into the present moment. Then she dismissed it.

Louise called the next day to ask Molly what the doctor had told her. Molly wouldn't talk about it. She hadn't been to the doctor yet, but she promised to go. She promised as though she were doing Louise a favor.

Dr. Slater did not confirm Louise's prediction. "You are not pregnant," he said, but Molly was so prepared for it that she felt a slight disappointment when she left his office. Her reasoning was faulty and romantic. Molly went to a nearby coffee shop, wanting to sit among strangers. She didn't want to give the impression of turmoil, so she walked with an imperious carriage. The spaces of memory inside her were provocations for regret, and she relegated to William more blame than he deserved.

Jill came by the house at ten o'clock that night. She worked late, but she wanted to see Molly and not hear the results over the phone.

"So?" She came in, slipped off one shoe, and let the other dangle from her toe. "What did he say?"

"It isn't true."

"Are you sorry?" Jill asked. "You look awful."

"You know what, Jill? I think that since Joe came home, I'm not sorry about anything." Molly took out a cigarette.

"Don't smoke that."

"Just one." She puffed on the cigarette, pretending not to inhale.

"Tell me what you thought would happen if it had been true. What are you imagining William would have said?"

Molly pulled up her shirt and stuck out her stomach to make it seem big. "I guess you're right," she said, as though she had given Jill a probable answer.

"Besides," Jill said, "what about Ben?"

The school year filled out into Christmas. Lucas ran guard on Lil Jack's All-Star Team. Lil Jack's was a pizza house run by the man who owned the mall. Franci entered her second semester of seventh grade with the haughtiness of having made it through the first humbling semester, and Joe won baseball games to become what amounted to a heroic pitcher in the spring. He lived half the time at his father's apartment, but kept his room, his clothes in the closet at home. He came home every day after school and usually ate dinner there.

Louise and Sig were written up in papers all over the state. Jill took much credit for their publicity, though her moves were guided and mentored by Frank Bates. Franci fell in love with Fred Jarelson and wore his gold chain and his shirts and jackets. He came to the house and they watched TV, or sometimes Ben or Molly dropped them at the movies, though usually Ben was asked to perform this rite since the idea of anybody's mother driving them anywhere was abominable.

The fall had gone silent as surely as the ending of the ringing of bells. The stupefaction of the sweet fall air gave a taciturn respect to winter. Winter with its deserted trees came in like a harsh white shadow and seared the ground with insult. The remedy for winter, thought Molly, was sleep, but her work increased. Asa wanted to see more paintings, and she felt the need to become diligent.

Ben came for regular dinners on Saturday and Thursday nights, though he often showed up on Monday and ate whatever was left over from the weekend. Sometimes he made a spaghetti recipe that had an excess of meat sauce but was a favorite dish. Once he tried a casserole of macaroni and vegetables, which didn't go over well,

though everyone ate as much as they could. Mainly, that night, they
ate a lot of bread.

The rainy months presaged the first green leaves, and summer
moved over them like a hot warehouse. The divorce papers were
being signed, but the children hadn't been told of this final action,
though their prescience about such matters made them progres-
sively impatient.

The summer went smoothly. They went to the beach again. Lucas brought Johnny along, and once they sneaked off with beer but
got caught by Joe. He took it away and presented them with a lecture
more severe than his father had given to him.

Fred Jarelson was at the beach the same week, so Franci spent
most of her time looking for him, or else in the room working to fix
her hair and get ready to look for him.

Ben and Molly had time alone, and Ben asked about the divorce.
It had been a year. More. And Molly's prognostication for herself
was still based in alarm. She pushed against the fevered delight she
felt with Ben. Sometimes she grew quiet and sulky.

During the year, Lucas developed impetigo, Franci caught the flu
five times, and Joe complained of a chronic stomachache. Once Joe's
complaints were severe enough to take him to the emergency room.
X-rays and a full workup showed that nothing was wrong. By sum-
mertime, a rhythm had defined itself around them, and Ben came
and went in the pattern of their lives with ease. Joe would be a senior
next year and referred to himself as "stud." He would try for schol-
arships in baseball or track.

Molly lived with the consolation of freedom and a silent peevish-
ness that was softened by Ben's steady pursuit. But Ben grew tired
of Molly's inexorable caution and told her, "You can be rude sometimes, Molly. Not only rude, you can be foolish." He wanted her to
understand what he meant, and he wanted to understand her—as
though loving had anything at all to do with understanding.

Molly didn't answer when Ben confronted her. Everything she
thought of to say sounded either rude or foolish. She bit her lip. His

heart was larger than hers, and she told him so. "My heart's nothing but string," she said, "a piece of string." Ben spoke with the urgency of a doctor who knows a cure. He put his arm around her. Molly loved the smell of his arms, like ripe fruit.

"Save a place for me at the picnic," he said.

When he said this simple statement—not a proclamation of love, but one request that indicated what they were in each other's lives— Molly was shocked to find how much time had gone by, and an improbable reason for love arose inside her.

"Will you?"

"I'll save it," she said, and she kissed him as though theirs was the visceral connection of many exhilarating years.

CHAPTER
TWELVE

What happened on the day of the town Founders' Day Picnic was impossible to predict. The picnic was always held the first weekend in October, and the entire town prepared for an all-day celebration. Everyone gathered three miles outside town beside the lake.

People came to the ridge as early as nine a.m. Each family claimed a spot of its own, much the same way as families claimed pews in an old church. Molly could tell who was present or absent by looking beside a particular tree or rock near the lake.

By midmorning most of the families were in place. The day was warm but the ground dry and dusty from lack of rain. Molly spread blankets and brought out a large bowl of pasta salad. By the time Ben showed up, it was almost noon, and he carried a bottle of her favorite wine.

Most of the afternoon passed in the languid hours designated for picnics. There were organized races and contests. The children set up lemonade stands and were guaranteed to make money at this gathering. Ben bought his third glass of lemonade from a little girl who considered him an easy mark, and Molly laughed with affection at his softness.

It was at that moment they saw a crowd gather at the edge of the lake. Someone yelled to someone else to come look, and the crowd gathered into a circle. The whole circle moved backward and forward together, like square dancers.

"What is it?" Ben yelled to Franci.

"A turtle," Lucas called back. "A big one."

"Don't get near it!" Molly tried to think if she'd ever had an occasion to warn them about snapping turtles before.

The turtle made its way out of the woods toward the lake. At times it stopped and drew its head and tail in. Finally, it settled into a muddy place and drew its whole self in.

The children went back to the diving rocks where they could jump from a high place into the lake. Lucas came to ask his mother's permission to jump from the rocks. "I'm old enough now," Lucas pleaded. "Johnny's mother said he could, and I'm older than Johnny by six months!"

"I guess so." Molly sat to keep an eye on what he did. "Where's Franci?"

Lucas pointed to the next person on the highest rock and Molly watched Franci perform a perfect dive, barely breaking the surface of the water as she entered it. She hadn't known Franci could dive so beautifully, and seeing it made her feel like a neglectful mother.

"Watch this!" Lucas ran. He jumped into the water, doing a belly flop on purpose. Those around him laughed. When his head came up, he looked to where his mother sat with Ben and waved. The way he did this left a string in Molly's heart. She gathered them now. She would make a new heart from all these strings.

Someone yelled, and Molly thought something else had happened with the turtle. But when she turned around she could see billows of smoke coming from the woods.

"There's a fire!"

The smoke came out from the trees, but the root of the fire was a shack in the middle of a clearing. Everyone fumbled to see it. The men ran toward the woods to do something, and the women looked around to make sure where their children were.

The shack was easy to see because of the clearing where it burned, a fairly contained fire, like a burning bush. The men could do nothing, because a trench had been dug around the shack and water from the lake poured through the trench. All of it had been a very deliberate task.

It was Zack's place. Molly knew that. It was deep enough in the woods and the trench had been carefully dug. What Molly did not know was whether or not he was inside.

A few men tried to jump the ditch to see if anyone lay trapped in the cabin, but the flames flew too high and too hot and most of the shack was destroyed. Anyone inside would be burned by now.

"This is Zack's," Molly said to Ben, or to anyone. She hadn't looked at anyone when she said it.

"He's with Louise and Sig though," Ben said.

An explosion punched everyone backwards and the final crash of the shack made the fire flare at first, then die down. The whole occurrence could have been destructive to the woods, but Zack had been too careful to let that happen. He'd spent days digging the trench, and when he found Molly at the waterfall, he had already begun these preparations. But that was one year ago.

Louise and Sig didn't suspect Zack's motives when he wished to come back to the Founders' Day Picnic. They let him take the truck, expecting him back that night.

He was found burned to a raw black, with only the barest evidence to tell who this man had been.

"Is it him?" Ben asked Molly.

No one answered or knew. The whole town knew about Isaac Belcher now. He had been working with Louise and Sig and any article about them always mentioned his name. Isaac was considered a success story.

They waited until the fire had burned all the way to the ground and then tried to clear away some of the hot boards and pieces of metal and tin.

Zack's hat, maybe it was his father's, lay beneath a bush on the other side of the trench. Molly imagined him sailing it across the trench before setting fire to all he had, and was.

The day Isaac Belcher saw Molly at the waterfall, he had pushed himself into a new position, which included beginning a trench around his house. He stopped when he saw Molly and Lucas behind the water, and he thought when he saw them that possibly the trench was not necessary, that a less drastic step could be considered. He hadn't thought of any of it as preparation for suicide. He hadn't thought of any technical terms for what he was doing. He just prepared as though he were getting ready for a storm, or a trip.

And that's exactly what happened. Because from the time he saw Molly and from the time he went into the hospital his mind forgot its plan. He let himself be lifted and carried, and when he ended up with Sig and Louise, his life took hold of itself and he couldn't even remember the days and months—years—at the shack, because he was over the fever that drove him.

But that fever emerged again when he went back for the Founders' Day picnic. He saw a large turtle sleeping in his house, taking it over with its smell. He drove out the turtle. He yelled, and kicked it until it moved toward the door and slowly out the back side of the trench toward the lake. He could not stand the old-fish smell of his shack. He decided to smoke it out, to build a fire and smoke the two rooms so the smell would be smoke instead of turtle.

But as Zack gathered small sticks and leaves and prepared a place in his stove to burn these things, his whole mind remembered the earlier plan. And when he remembered, memory became stronger than present life, taking everything over. The old plan worked in his head like the turtle smell. The regular life he had at Sig's was not strong enough to erase what he was. For Isaac Belcher, the regular life was not yet his own, but this shack and his own early years and the smell of the turtle were real.

So he poured the kerosene he had put aside for this occasion, and he placed himself in the middle of the first room. When he lit a match to it, even at that moment he thought he would see Louise and Sig again, so confused was his tracing of time. He thought he was burning this part of his life, and that the new part could stay intact. He thought he could undo what had happened in his early years, but he didn't recognize that without his past times, his present times had no life either. He didn't realize any of this when he lit the match, or when he saw and heard the flames rush toward the roof.

Some of the children at the diving rock heard it first. They said, "What was that?" because they heard a sound like a soft explosion, and one child saw a flash of light in the woods, but no one did anything about it then.

A few minutes later, a woman near the lake yelled that there was a fire in the woods. The children thought she was calling them again to see the turtle or something about the turtle, but she yelled that there was a fire, and the men came running.

"The burial will be next week," Molly told her father when she called him. She couldn't believe Zack was dead. She didn't even know all he had become to her. Frank Bates said he would come for the funeral. He asked Molly how she was.

"He was burned so badly. I don't know what they can find to bury." She didn't know another way to speak about it. "I'll be glad to see you," she said.

The divorce had gone through, papers signed, and Molly told her father about that now. It was a dreaded and failed moment, as she told him.

"Have you talked with William?" Her father had asked her to speak with William, to discuss how they should present this to Joe and Franci and Lucas. He expected them to talk about things as though they were still married. He asked again, "Have you spoken with him?"

"Not yet."

"Molly!" He spoke as though she were six years old and he had told her to close the door.

That night Molly dreamed, though much of the dream had actually happened when she was a child. It was early summer and almost seven o'clock. Her father had finished making a doll he worked on for many weeks. Each day when he came home from work he asked where Molly was and told her, "You've never had anything like this." She would jump into his arms. She would never again feel the kind of affection she received during those weeks. All of this part was true.

In the dream Molly didn't know he was making a doll, she only knew from the perspective of the dreamer, and she had both perspectives in this dream. On the afternoon he finished it, he stepped through shadows across the yard and the child Molly sat on the ground and watched him walk through light and shadow—appear, disappear, appear.

He handed the doll to her. It was made of soft rags, but the head was a carved piece of blond wood, and that was the part that had taken him so long to make. All of this was true.

He carved a face into the wood. The eyes were cut-out holes with marbles that could roll around inside the head. The marbles, streaked on one side, made the doll look blind sometimes. But if Molly rolled the marbles with her finger to the dark solid side, the doll had the look of intense disturbance. The change could happen in seconds. All of this was true too, though in the dream the doll was a strange and ugly creature, and that part was not true.

The doll's lashes, above and below the marbles, were thick. They were the glamorous eyes of someone older, but the doll was a baby doll and glamorous eyes were out of place. None of this was true. The hair was sewn together and glued on. It swooped up in back like a tail.

But the most astonishing feature was the mouth, which was open slightly, as though it were about to speak. Her father said it was supposed to be a smile, but he pointed to show Molly what glimmered

there inside. She looked in to find ten tiny teeth stuck into the
wooden gums. The final effect was terrible, and this was the impertinence of the dream—her father had pulled out the teeth of dead
animals with tweezers and had placed them carefully in the doll's
mouth.

Molly loved the doll, in the dream and in life. In the dream,
though, she even loved the odd teeth. To see them there was thrill-
ing. To see them made her feel the doll had actual blood.

Molly jumped into her father's arms when he gave it to her, and
she woke as she jumped. But when she woke it was still the middle
of the night and a light shone into her room, on her bed, a street light,
something, but she didn't recognize it. It was not white, but a yel-
lowish color, not the shape of a whole moon, but almost round. It
was too large for a streetlight and too high in the sky, so Molly knew
it must be the moon, but still she didn't recognize it. What had her
father done that made her not recognize the moon? She thought she
knew it by heart.

The next morning she woke as suddenly as she had when she
jumped into her father's arms, and she knew just as suddenly that if
she could feel loved by her father, she could feel loved by anyone.

Molly approached William's office with a dry buzzing sound in her
head. She didn't know what she expected to say to him. She had
called to say she would come by, and he suggested she come to the
office. Molly agreed to meet him there. He said to come in the late
afternoon.

She hadn't visited his office in over a year and she didn't recognize
the plush carpet in the hall. It smelled new. The secretary, too, was
new and didn't know Molly, so Molly introduced herself, not saying
she was William's wife, but saying her name to let the secretary
make the connection.

When William opened the door to his office, she couldn't help
being struck by the change she noticed in him. His demeanor was
one of success—all around him nodding heads, admiring glances,

prizes from a fat world. But the most complete change was in the guarded expression of his face and in his gestures. His gestures were familiar, but his hands were the hands of a stranger.

They made polite exchanges, until Molly asked if she seemed different to him. He told her yes, she had changed. Molly took a deep breath.

"Zack Belcher's funeral is tomorrow."

"I know. I saw the shack. But he'd moved in with the Penrys, hadn't he?" William offered Molly coffee and asked if she was hungry, but he couldn't give more than politeness. "What did you want to see me about, Molly?"

Molly shifted. She wanted to tell how she had loved him, and she wanted to say she loved Ben, how all these fractions had been curative. "I don't know how to say it."

William waited.

"Will, on that night we grieved for Joe . . ." William did not want to remember it now. "When we were together." She hadn't meant to ever tell him this. "Will, I thought I was pregnant after that night."

If he had leaned toward her, or if he had pulled away, if he had moved at all, she might have known what to do. But he didn't move. He sat as if everything might break if he moved. Molly felt paralyzed inside their stillness, so that for a moment they both looked as if they waited for a poisonous snake to crawl back into its hole.

When William finally moved, he tried to smile, but it was the smile of a blind man. Both of them struggled to do something with their mouths.

"Molly." The fact that he said her name in a soft way made all the difference. "Is that what you wanted to say?" He didn't trust this to be all.

"And the other thing," Molly said, speaking as though this were an offhand remark, "is that everything is final now. I got the papers in the mail."

"I did too." He tried to confide something more personal than he knew how to say, or think. "This is best, Molly. We don't love each other anymore."

"I keep forgetting," she said.

"But I don't regret that night, I won't ever regret it."

Molly made a motion with her hand to imply that what he said meant more than she knew how to convey.

"I've thought," he said, "you know, I've thought how maybe it actually brought Joe back. In some way brought him back." His eyes looked excited with the power he felt saying it.

Will. Molly didn't say his name but thought it out loud from the heart. This seed in old ground whose habit was to flourish. She didn't know if she should touch his arm or what.

"There's nothing more to say. Anyway, Molly," and he spoke now about the present moment, "you want to tell Lucas and Franci?"

Molly nodded. "Yes. I'll do that." She waited, thinking. "Will you be at Zack's funeral?"

"Yes. You want to sit together?"

"No." She would sit with Ben.

"Listen, " he said, his voice lower, as though this were his real voice and before he had been acting, "I want to tell Joe myself."

William followed her to the elevator, but then rode down and followed her to the parking lot too. The whole force of his body appeared in disarray. His tie was askew, and sad.

But the sadness for them both was buried in all they had not known. They didn't know how love could end or, if not ended, could collapse upon them. They didn't know how they could fool themselves about what happiness was, and how they thought they could reach it with such ease. Their grief was personal, but their sadness had more to do with their own amazing ignorance about ways of loving.

In the parking lot William stood beside Molly's car and tried to decide if he should kiss her goodbye. Neither of them knew what was appropriate anymore. In one way, everything seemed appropriate; in another way, nothing did. The sun on William's hair showed grey and looked like ice in places. Molly almost mentioned this to him, but was afraid it might sound too intimate. She wanted to touch his shirt. It looked rumpled and soft like bedclothes, and he gazed at her as though he were looking at fire.

Molly kissed him quickly and started the car. She said something, made some slight comment, but as she drove off couldn't think of what she had said. She decided not to look in the rearview mirror. She didn't want to see him walk toward the building, his coatless back. She would not lift her eyes to see.

But she did see. All of it—the slant of sun, his reasonable stride, the look of refusal when he stood beside the car and turned and said to no one, "Don't you understand anything? Don't you understand anything at all?"

On the next afternoon Joe came home from school early enough to find his mother in the garden. She was putting in bulbs for next spring. He stood around while she asked him questions and then said, "Dad told me."

"I haven't told Lucas and Franci yet."

"That's what I figured."

"What do you think?" Molly asked, but immediately thought, what a question. She couldn't take it back. She had wanted it to sound casual.

"He told me about the night when you thought I was dead." So Joe knew what they had done to keep him alive, and he liked being the cause of such a phenomenon. He couldn't say any of this to his mother. "I'm going to stay here tonight," he said. "I miss sleeping in my own bed."

Franci went with her mother to the airport to pick up Papa Frank. The plane was an hour late, so they stood where they could watch the planes. Franci talked about school and Fred Jarelson. Fred loved someone else now.

"I don't know what I should *do*," Franci said. She'd thought this, but hadn't said it out loud. She moped around the house and memorized more sentences from her book. She decided to tell her mother the name of the book.

"Finally," said Molly.

"Those volumes you keep in your studio—*The Notebooks of Leonardo da Vinci*." She spoke as if this were a joke on her mother.

"You went in there to look through them?"

"I used to do it all the time, but not much anymore. He wrote down some wild things."

Molly liked that Franci sneaked into her studio to study the da Vinci volumes. "What would he say about Fred Jarelson now? If you looked up something that might give you advice, what would it be?"

"I already did."

"And?"

"*The hare is so timid and scared that he even runs from leaves that fall off the trees in autumn.*"

"What does that have to do with Fred?"

"Fred is the hare."

Papa Frank walked up in front of them. They had missed hearing his flight arrival called, and he teased them about it. He hugged Franci first. No one mentioned Zack until they got to the car.

"Did you come for Zack's funeral?" Franci asked.

"Only partly," he said, and looked to Molly.

"I talked to him," Molly said, meaning she had talked with William about the divorce, "but not to anyone else." Then she said, "Joe knows."

"*I* know." Franci thought they talked about the fire, or else the turtle. She was guessing.

Molly smiled at Papa Frank and spoke over Franci's head. "Franci knows everything. Just ask what new wisdom she has."

"What new wisdom do you have?"

"*Dust makes damage.*"

"A truth if I ever heard one."

"What do *you* have?"

"Two, actually, but I'll give you one now." He handed her a piece of paper with a sentence written on it.

"She told me where they came from," Molly bragged.

Papa Frank looked at Franci. "She told *me* a long time ago."

CHAPTER

THIRTEEN

What seemed strange was the way people came to Isaac Belcher's funeral. He was buried in the church cemetery, and most of Stringer's Ridge came to help bury him.

Louise and Sig drove from Shelby and brought all their children, dressed in Sunday clothes. Zack had not been upset or depressed when he left in their truck, they said. Maybe when he went to his shack he saw the trench and was reminded of his former plan— which had changed now, but had not changed enough.

Molly criticized herself. She tried to think of what she should have done.

"No one could've stopped this, Molly." Sig had been to the coroner. They had decided to put Zack's remains in a bag and bury him without trying to clean him up. So much of his skin was gone, and in places the skeleton showed through. Sig was shocked at how little of his body was left to bury.

The day before the funeral Molly went to see what was left of the shack and she walked around its remains. She studied the trench and the surrounding area. The turtle had come back to its resting place.

Its head and boggled eyes, framed by its own weight, seemed old, an old dream in a slower earth form.

When Zack decided to stay at Louise and Sig's, it was a decision based on his wish to take care of the horses. He had had that job as a boy. He worked in a stable where he learned to ride for the price of keeping stalls clean, feeding the horses, and tending to their minor cuts and sores. He was so adept at this that the veterinarian trusted Zack to do more and more. And Zack received extra pay for his work.

But all that came to an end. Zack's father called the barn one day and the owner bragged about Zack—his intelligence and perseverance. The father had worked in the same mill for thirty-five years and hated the idea that his son might surpass him, might even become a doctor for horses. So he forced Zack out of the stable, and found a job for him at the mill.

For a while Zack could sneak to the stables at lunchtime or after work and see the horses, feel and smell their soft brown coats, rub them down. He did this without pay. The owner sympathized and tried to think of another way Zack could come to the barn. He offered a Saturday job and called the father to say he was shorthanded and could Zack come on Saturday mornings. "It's a busy time for us," he said, "we could use him." So Zack went to work at the stables on Saturdays, but his father questioned him when he came in, asking what he had done and making sure that Zack's training could never take him far away.

Zack had already guessed what his father would do, and he took precautions so that it wouldn't happen, but the happening came in the middle of the night, as Zack slept in a bed next to his mother's old sewing room. She had been gone from the house for fifteen years. Zack was seventeen the year he worked at the stable.

He got up early one Saturday morning and went into the kitchen. There was no sign of his father being up, and he was glad of that. He hoped he could eat and get out the door before the old man woke.

He did. He got out the door and even let the screen door slam, but no sound came from his father's bedroom, so he drove his truck to the barn three miles away. He could not believe his good luck at not waking his father, and as he rode his mood was lighter and finer than it had been in months. He was beginning to think kind thoughts about his father, as he did sometimes, but the thoughts were more connected to his own mood and to the brightness of the day.

The barn too was bright and still as his truck made its way to the side where he always parked, but as he got out he could see, in one of the stalls, a horse's left hoof on the ground and blood moving from under the stall's door. The whole scene did not register immediately in Zack's mind, and he went slowly into the stall.

The horse lay on its side. It was not dead, not quite dead. When Zack looked in, the horse raised his head slightly, but much blood had been lost and there was no strength left even to cry out.

Two of its legs were cut off at the first joint, and blood gathered in a dark puddle around him. Zack kept his composure, but knew immediately all that had happened, though he didn't imagine the extent of it. He knew his father had been here and that this performance was his—Zack had seen him at other times do such things to animals caught in traps in the woods. He would take an animal out of the trap and cut off a leg or a foot, or more than one, and look at the animal wobble and search for a way to stand without pain. His father, when he first did this, laughed at the animal as though he laughed at something drunk, but as the behavior continued through the years he stopped laughing and watched with a concentration that Zack saw nowhere else in his life.

There were nights when Zack wondered if his father might perform such a thing on him. Seeing this, one stall after another of mutilation, he wished it *had* been on himself. He thought that if it had been himself, these horses could have gone unharmed.

Then Zack heard a high-pitched noise like a whine, but not from a horse. He turned around and saw his father going toward the truck. He heard again the whine, but then knew it came from the deep part of his own throat and that it was connected to a vague, far-off wish about his father.

So Isaac Belcher did this—he took a coathanger that lay on the ground and he went toward his father in blindness, and his father, who hadn't gotten into the truck, didn't see Zack, so much was he into his own absurd plan. And with the coathanger Zack cut his father's neck. He jerked or jabbed the sharp end into his neck as the father turned to see the son, and it went into the middle soft place of the neck, the place Zack's mother liked to kiss when they were younger. "Your mother always liked to kiss me here," his father sometimes said, pointing to the cupped place between the two clavicle bones.

And the rusty piece went straight in, until his father yelled out, but without making any noise. And there was more blood, but this time Zack thought that no one in the county would convict him of anything against this heinous man. Though he didn't think anything just then, he only felt the coathanger push into the soft flesh, and heard a foul cry before the tumbling occurred—a thrust of the father's arms upward to clasp at something, his own breath, or some other way to breathe. His whole body flung up into Isaac's face, to be speechless and hidden in his mind.

His father fell, still scooting around for breath. He stopped then, and the gasps he gave seemed more unconscious than the horse Zack had just seen. And Zack thought how his father was luckier than the horses, because he was dying and going into an unconscious state so quickly.

The owner came out, wild-eyed, because he had been there as it happened but couldn't stop Zack's crazed father, and now the wild-eyed owner wanted to do something that matched what had been done, but Zack had already finished it. So they stood over the father and were silent. Anyone coming up at that moment would have thought they were praying, so solemn were their faces and so intent on some spiritual word that could absolve them from this scene.

It was this image Isaac Belcher carried into reform school, and through all the years until he was twenty-seven.

He stayed at Louise and Sig's for almost a year, but he was never convinced that his life there was real. There could be nothing ever as real as that day at the barn with his father and the horses he had tried to heal and the owner who took Zack in for a short time during the trial.

Zack had told all this to Sig and told it again to Louise. He hadn't told it since the time of the trial, and Sig listened, but not with an eye for justice. He listened with tears of consolation. Sig picked up books on veterinary practice and brought them to Zack. He and Louise offered the beginnings of a new life, but Zack couldn't believe it at all. He lived with the thought that all of this could happen again.

The people of the town dressed up to bury their stranger. They read about Zack in the newspaper. On the day he was buried, the paper printed another article about the time he spent at the Penrys. They wrote of his work with horses.

The minister spoke of those who were strangers in the town, those without homes, of this man's life, and life without hope. It sounded like a sermon and was personal because this man's death was so impersonal. Some of the people cried for themselves, but some cried for Zack.

Just before the final hymn, Sig went to the podium where the minister stood and he motioned that he wanted to say "just one thing."

And Sig told them the story of Zack as close as he could to the way Zack had told him. "Some asked me if I thought he was dangerous, if to have him around was dangerous. I think it probably was. To have anyone among us who hasn't had even one regular experience of being loved is potentially a dangerous thing."

The town heard the exaggerated violence of Isaac Belcher and his father, and it touched their own violent nature with intense rapture. So Isaac became a metaphor of possibility for their own lives.

Sig didn't know as he told it what the story would become. He had no intention but to personally introduce the young Isaac who had grown into the man everyone knew. But as they left the burial, everyone knew something more about themselves.

Isaac burned the shack and himself in it. In doing so he unleashed the town's own burning. When they found his body, they stood clear of the fire because it was too hot, but they also stood clear of Isaac.

"I see children burning with the same fever as Isaac," Sig told them. "Sometimes these children are forty or sixty, sometimes they are eight or five years old. The way you recognize them is by the look of ambush in their faces."

Sig spoke to the crowd, some standing, some sitting on benches or chairs. He stood there, and his chin quivered until Louise came up and led him off.

People didn't know just what he meant, but as they went home that night, each family thought about Sig's speech. And for several days they felt inspired as a town, but the curious effect of it died down, and they worked themselves back into a muscular intelligence which allowed their lives to go unchanged. The empty air settled again into temporary space around them and all organizations went on as though Isaac Belcher had never been born.

Molly lifted her eyes from the letter she was writing. She hadn't written anything in several long minutes but stared at the dark red fabric of the chair opposite her. The room was full of shadows from a light defined by the lampshade on the table.

Yesterday, after the burial, she came into this room to be alone, but Franci came in with her, not to interrupt anything she was doing, just to have company as she had done on the nights when sleepwalking brought her to her mother's room. She sat huddled in the dress she had worn all day.

Molly didn't utter a word when Franci came in, and Franci didn't need any word from her. She stayed for a length of time, but left, and that was the moment Molly picked up a pen and paper to write Franci a letter. It would be to Joe and Lucas too, though she addressed it to Franci:

Dear Franci,
Sometimes there is more to tell you than I know how to say, so I pick up the pen to try what is so difficult. If I could change the way we are with each other, I would make a different climate for you. I would lengthen each day and keep you from wishing for things you might lose. I would make the pain of loving Fred Jarelson disappear. But all of this would be wrong.

What we wish for is more than just wish. It's not what we lose, but how we start again. Zack forgot that. Your dad and I forgot too—in all the ignorant ways we tried to repair ourselves. Our stumbling, awkward dance couldn't be fashioned into smooth steps.

When Joe was ten, he thought the way he understood things was completely right. We all think this at every age, but never so much as at ten. And he expressed himself easily, then, in song and the making-up of stories. Over the next years, the climate of our house did such violence to his mood, and I see the result of what we did. What I don't know is what is lost in you and in Lucas. I don't know the wounds that will keep you from doing all you can do.

Oh, Franci, have I said yet in all of this that I love you? Have I said it enough in your whole life, for you to know that, among all the mistakes and omissions, that to forget to say this is the worst? Have I said that your whole spirit as you grow older occupies my heart in such a way that makes my chest cavity the size and weight of a bowling ball? And that I give that same bowling-ball-heart to Lucas and one to Joe, and sometimes I can't figure how to have room for my own wispy breathing?

I will give you this letter, because I have written it and don't know what else to do.

But Molly didn't give it to her. She decided instead to try to tell them in some other way. She would wait until Halloween, when they would feel excited and happy.

Lucas and Johnny said they wanted to sleep all night in the tree house. Just the two of them, they said.

"All night?" Molly hoped they would stay out there just until twelve or one.

"We want it to be all night," said Johnny. He didn't look at Molly. Johnny hardly ever looked straight at anyone.

Friday was the night. The moon was not full, part of it covered, and Lucas couldn't look at it without thinking of the eclipse.

Molly gave them extra blankets and two lunch sacks full of food—sandwiches, chips, popcorn, and two Cokes wrapped in aluminum foil to keep them cold. They had two flashlights, which were kept turned on so that the treehouse looked like a room.

By twelve o'clock they had finished wandering the neighborhood and settled themselves into their blankets and bedrolls, when Johnny said, "I hear something."

Lucas heard it too, but hadn't said anything. They listened.

"What is it?" Johnny stuck his head out the hole that was a window. "Hey!" A scrabbling went all along the roof and side and Johnny bumped his head, saying words Lucas knew but wasn't allowed to say.

"It's a raccoon," Lucas yelled. He saw him run down the tree. "He wants the food probably."

"Give it to him."

Lucas dropped a sack of food to the ground. They saw the raccoon eat everything. He tasted one thing, then another, as though it were hard to decide.

"We'd never've seen this if we hadn't been outside," said Johnny, and Lucas could tell this was a big moment for Johnny, but he didn't know why.

"If my dad were here, I'd tell him about this." Johnny lay down as if it were over.

"It's just twelve-thirty," Lucas said.

"You should tell *your* dad," Johnny urged.

"I will." Lucas thought about when he would tell him and if anybody else would be around. "He built this treehouse, you know." He was trying to give his dad some credit.

The raccoon climbed back up the tree and across the roof. He looked into the window hole at them, as close as a few feet from Johnny's bed.

"Watch out for rabies!" Johnny said. It was something his mother had warned him about.

"He just wants more food," said Lucas, and Johnny threw out the other sack. They watched the raccoon open it with his handlike paws.

"He's almost human!" Johnny said.

"Yeah," but Lucas didn't think he was anywhere near human.

"What'll we do if he comes back?" Johnny asked.

"Just let him come in, look around." They could hear him climbing the tree again. He came through the window hole and walked across Johnny to the other side. Johnny felt brave from the experience of feeling the raccoon's feet on his blanket.

The next morning, Lucas woke first. In the corner next to Johnny the raccoon lay asleep. Crackles of sunlight came through the boards and looked like light on water.

"Johnny." Lucas touched him lightly, but the raccoon heard and scooted out. Johnny woke to the sound of the claws, and even though he was half-asleep, he knew what it was.

"Ahh-hhh," he yelled, as though he were about to be hurt.

"He slept up here with us."

"Man!"

"He slept near you, near your feet."

"Oh, man!" All of this they could tell to people all day, but Johnny was thinking of how to tell his dad.

CHAPTER
FOURTEEN

Lucas heard his mother speaking to Jill on the porch. He hadn't meant to overhear. Usually Lucas didn't notice what grownups said, even if he was in the same room, or even if they spoke directly to him. But his ears picked up the tone of urgency as Jill spoke to his mother.

"You *have* to tell them that it's final, Molly."

"I don't know how they'll take it."

"Don't wait much longer. They would want to know this."

Lucas came out to the porch. It was easy to pretend he hadn't heard anything. The music that ended "The Flintstones" played, and Jill asked about his teacher. Lucas didn't want to talk about Mrs. Gastes but told them he thought he'd seen the fox, once or maybe twice. He said he was sure it was Fire, because he recognized the way it ran.

"Franci went to look too, but we couldn't find him again." He explained how Franci went by herself and came back saying she'd seen him and knew where he lived now. Lucas described to them the particular place. He didn't know why he was telling them this. What he wanted was for them to tell *him* something. He wanted to say, "Tell me, tell me."

The next day was Saturday, but Lucas didn't watch the Saturday morning cartoons anymore, or rather he'd grown more selective. He watched "Megawars" and "Knight Rider" before deciding to go to the stream. The morning had a cool fog. The rain felt misty and had the chill of fall, and though the stream was not full, it kept a steady, restorative murmur.

He went to where he knew the crate was. It stayed lodged between two rocks, but there were only two or three boards left. He pulled the boards loose and threw them into the creek—threw them as if they were bones. That is how things were. He hadn't seen his dad in two weeks.

The mist quickly changed into rain, but Lucas didn't care. He felt like an animal in the woods. He grew soaked and thought about how tall he was. He couldn't remember. He held out his arm to remember how long it was. Franci had measured his arms and legs one day. "Your right arm is one and a half feet long," she said. He wanted to think of numbers.

The rain grew worse and as Lucas started home he began to run. He slipped twice and water filled his shoes and socks. It was still early when he went into the house. He ran into his mother's room, pulled back her covers, and climbed into the bed.

"What in the world!" Molly jumped up. Lucas told her nothing. He shivered and soaked her bed with rainwater.

"Look at you! You're soaking wet."

Still he said nothing, because he thought he owed her nothing. He thought she owed him everything.

"Where have you been?"

He didn't answer.

She hadn't suggested that he take off his clothes, she hadn't suggested anything. She let him lie beside her, then got up to run a hot bath. He didn't object. His wet clothes soaked her gown and sheets, and he wouldn't speak a word. He lay beside her, folded, like a small rag.

The next night Lucas woke with a fever. He cried with restlessness, and Molly called the doctor to describe the symptoms. He asked what medicines she had.

"Tylenol, aspirin. Shouldn't we have something stronger?" She wanted the doctor to come over. Lucas had a temperature of 103°. She listened carefully to the instructions about bathing Lucas in tepid water and cooling him down with wet towels. She was to call back if the fever kept climbing.

Franci heard Lucas crying. "What's the matter with him? He looks like he can't wake up."

"He has a fever." She prepared a bath of tepid water.

"What're you going to do?"

"We have to cool him off." Molly gave Franci a small bowl and towel and told her to wash his face.

They placed Lucas in the tub, but left his underwear on. Franci poured cups of water onto his shoulders and chest. They put him back into bed, but in thirty minutes filled the tub again. Franci kept getting dry underwear for him, though finally they put him in without underwear. He didn't seem to care. Franci had seen him without underwear before. She had seen him naked, but she hadn't seen him not care. She felt ashamed for him.

"I'm going to call Ben," Molly said.

It was four-thirty when Ben came over. "You look worse than Lucas," Ben told her. Lucas slept now without fitfulness. "You and Franci lie down on the other bed," said Ben.

"Every fifteen minutes," Molly said. "I check his temperature every fifteen minutes."

The next time Molly woke, it was morning and she could smell breakfast cooking. Lucas' arms and head were no longer hot. Molly went to teach her class at ten o'clock and Ben stayed home with Lucas. When Molly got home she found them playing gin rummy and five card stud. They used Sweet Tarts as money.

They were getting ready for Halloween, going to buy a pumpkin. But first they would put flowers on Zack's grave. They were no sooner out the door than Franci said, "You remember the Sunday afternoon when we were playing on the volleyball court at Johnny's house?"

Molly said she did.

"And somebody, you or Dad, called us in and said we were going out to dinner because you hadn't had time to make anything?"

Molly didn't remember saying it, but guessed she had. She didn't remember any details about the day Franci spoke of, only the larger setting.

"And when we got in the house Joe said what was the matter and you said, nothing, but we didn't believe it. Dad looked sick. I thought he had been sick. Anyway, that night I bawled. I couldn't think what about. I kept thinking about what I wanted to be when I grew up. I couldn't think of something I could be."

Everything Franci said was in the nature of a question. She wore a heavy furry sweater and looked like a stuffed package. "It was like, it was like," she searched for a likeness, "like the house smelled sick, and like some old, old person had gotten so sick that we couldn't talk or anything, couldn't be the way we used to be, or if we were loud, it would be worse than if we had been too loud a year ago. So I bawled, but I did it in bed. Just Lucas heard me."

"What did Lucas do?"

"He said what was wrong, just asking over and over, 'What's wrong, Franci?' and I kept saying, 'Just everything,' so he stopped asking and went back to his room."

Molly felt blank of head. What she struggled so hard to get hold of was a slight chance of knowing what one thing means. One action, one remembered image, one gesture, a house and its smell that changes in an afternoon.

Franci had learned more at her young age than Molly knew now. They laid pink and white flowers on Zack's grave, and Molly felt a white stone flicker brought back into her life. The season was changing, the leaves expressing a canopy of color on the landscape. The wind blew cool, and she and Franci stood for a long while pointing to clouds that changed quickly into wisps or chunky rabbit shapes.

Halloween was on Sunday, and even the air in Stringer's Ridge seemed orange. The house had the mood of Christmas expectation, because a big dinner was planned for five o'clock. Louise came at noon with the twins. She brought a small sewing machine and set it up in the bedroom, taking sheets and old clothes to turn into fantastic costumes. She felt like a magician, she said.

Franci designed (though Louise figured out how to make it) a Queen Elizabeth costume from an old sheet and a blanket and a piece of cardboard used to make a high, stiff collar. The sleeves fit tightly around the wrists and gave a puffiness to her shoulders. Lucas said it was funny-looking. The skirt wasn't full enough, but the way it was gathered at the waist had the effect of fullness. Joe made a crown for her, and when she said she needed a scepter, Lucas let her borrow his snake stick, or what he called his snake stick.

He carried the stick whenever he went to the woods, in case he came across a snake. Lucas knew about snakes. He knew the names and descriptions of all the poisonous ones. Once he lifted a harmless green snake and it crawled along the stick toward him. He felt brave and kept the stick on the wall in his room. He let Franci use this stick and hoped she might write something about it in her diary. He wrapped it in aluminum foil and formed a knob at the end that meant she could bestow blessings, or whatever it was queens did.

Joe and Lucas carved a pumpkin and took suggestions from anyone who wanted to enter the process. Louise told them to make the eyes slanted instead of round, so they did. Franci told them to put in lots of teeth. Molly said to put newspaper underneath everything and to clean up the mess when they were through. She said to draw or cut eyebrows. "Eyebrows make it scary."

Jill came over and brought a pumpkin pie. Joe and Lucas called her to the porch to see their carving. They asked what her costume would be.

"You'll see." She spoke with unusual secrecy.

"Ben will come later," Molly said to Jill. Jill counted chairs for people who would be there for supper. "He'll be here for dessert."

Franci sashayed around the house in her long queen's costume, and Lucas wore his pirate's outfit all day. "Johnny wants to eat with us," he said, and Molly said, "Tell Meatball he can come too. Tell him Joe will be here."

Lucas had Molly paint a skull and crossbones on both of his arms, like tattoos. He wore his hat sideways and made a dagger out of cardboard and foil. The twins did not want to make their costumes and instead chose box skeletons from the drugstore.

"That's what they wanted," Louise said without apology. They chose skeletons so you couldn't tell which was the boy and which the girl.

Louise wore a Gypsy fortune-teller costume made out of bright scarves and a Mexican skirt. She wore bangles on her wrists and ankles that made a jangling noise everywhere she went. Jill appeared in a dark leotard and a horse's head to put over her own.

"I can't eat in this thing, but I wanted to wear it." It was for Zack. Her costume was for him. Nobody mentioned it, and maybe only Molly and Louise realized it, but the others appreciated Jill's appearance in her tight leotard and her graceful galloping around the kitchen.

Lucas followed Jill, galloping behind her, then Franci in a more gentle strut. The twins and Louise came into the dance, then Molly moved in behind them herself, her soft feet pacing the twins. Joe cheered and clapped and helped them keep a rhythm to their steps. And for a moment Molly saw them all moving in perfect balance.

Molly had not put on her costume yet—a clown suit. She went to her room to get it. She wore sweat pants tied at the ankles so the legs would balloon out, and she did the same with a shirt, tying the wrists so it would be full in the arms. She found shoes too big for her and made up her face with white powder. She drew eyes to look larger than normal and exaggerated her smile by drawing paint up the side of her cheeks toward her ears. She let her hair go wild around her. When she came downstairs, all the food sat steaming on the table.

Joe wore an authentic Indian vest and had painted his face like a chieftain's. He announced that he would sit at the end of the table where William used to sit.

Johnny and Meatball disguised themselves as robots. They wore cardboard boxes and let their legs stick out. They had silvered their legs.

"Before we eat," Molly said, "I have something I want to say."

Lucas wailed. "Is this going to take *long*?" He took a roll unbuttered and offered one to Johnny. "I'm *hungry*."

"You make a good clown, Mama," Franci said. She had the look of someone who knew what her mother would say and was asking her not to say it now. "Let's just go ahead and eat."

"I want to explain just *one* thing." Molly had already prepared for this moment and found it difficult to throw out now.

"See? It *is* going to take long."

They got into position to listen politely, and Molly began to speak in metaphor. She described the physical structure of constellations and everyone seemed to be listening. But when Ben came in, Molly knew they were bored because they acted so glad to see him and tried to change the subject.

Ben pulled up a chair. He was the only one not in costume, so Lucas gave him the pirate hat to wear during dinner. It was too small. Ben wore it anyway.

"Mama's telling us something," Franci said. She wanted to get on with it. They grew quiet again.

The configuration of table and the constellation of forms sat before Molly like a pattern too close to describe. Nothing she could imagine was as strong as the constellation already here before her: an Elizabethan queen, two small skeletons, the Gypsy fortune-teller, an Indian chieftain, silver-legged robots, a pirate, one sleek horse, Ben with the too-small skull-and-bones hat, and herself a bright clown. So she announced that the final legal papers had gone through. Just said it.

"I wanted you to know," she said. No one seemed surprised.

"But what does that *mean*?" said Lucas.

Franci gave the red skeleton some salad on his/her plate, and Molly took comfort in the movement of her daughter's arms at that moment. She took comfort in the slow change of constellations, knowing what was in the sky tonight, and tomorrow night, and in the winter. She knew other things, but she didn't speak her thoughts. Instead she sang a blessing from her childhood, the Gloria Patri:

"As it wa-as in the be-gin-ning . . ." It was short and no one joined in the singing because they hadn't expected it and because it didn't sound like a regular blessing.

"But I don't know what that _means_."

"It means they're divorced," said Joe.

Lucas pushed back from the table. His chair balanced on two legs, and he leaned forward in a precarious position.

"It _means_," said Franci. She looked at them all at once, as someone does before an announcement.

Lucas' chair came down with a loud, scraping halt.

"It means that it's not over yet." Franci felt the force of those sitting around her. She knew how they would all go on loving.

The Gypsy passed the potatoes to the two skeletons and the robots offered a roll to the Elizabethan queen. This table had the excitement now of a special eve, and everyone was still hungry.